THE PARENT PROBLEM

Anna Wilson

Illustrated by Nicola Kinnear

MACMILLAN CHILDREN'S BOOKS

First published 2016 by Macmillan Children's Books
an imprint of Pan Macmillan
20 New Wharf Road, London N1 9RR
Associated companies throughout the world
www.panmacmillan.com

ISBN 978-1-5098-0131-2

Text copyright © Anna Wilson 2016
Illustrations copyright © Nicola Kinnear 2016

The right of Anna Wilson and Nicola Kinnear to be identified as the author
and illustrator of this work has been asserted by them in accordance
with the Copyright, Designs and Patents Act 1988.

1 3 5 7 9 8 6 4 2

A CIP catalogue record for this book is available from
the British Library.

Printed and bound by CPI Group (UK) Ltd, Croydon CR0 4YY

For my dear dad, Martin Hankey,
who passed away during the writing of this book.
Thank you, Dad, for all your silly songs, funny jokes
and crazy stories. We miss you every day.

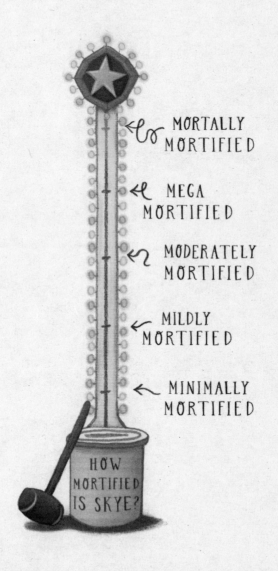

MORTALLY
MORTIFIED

MEGA
MORTIFIED

MODERATELY
MORTIFIED

MILDLY
MORTIFIED

MINIMALLY
MORTIFIED

HOW
MORTIFIED
IS SKYE?

The ~~Chronicles~~ *Mortifying life* of Skye Green

I have always wanted to write a book. I write a journal already (this is it) and I like to think that one day someone will find my diary and publish it. Maybe when I am as dead (and famous) as Charles Dickens or Roald Dahl or Astrid Lindgren (if you don't know who she is, look her up – she is awesome). But I would really like to have something published before I die, so that is why I have decided to write a novel.

I have been a bookworm since probably forever and I think that being a writer must be the best job in the world. I mean, you get PAID for living inside your imagination. What could be better than that?

Trouble is, it turns out that putting your imagination on to the page so that other people can read your brilliant, creative ideas is harder than you might think. I find, for example, that my brain is overflowing with great stories and insightful observations while I am staring out of the bus window on my way home from school. However, as soon as I get home and open a notebook and try to get the ideas down on paper, everything seems to evaporate, and I am left doodling in the margins, or scribbling 'I CAN'T THINK OF ANYTHING TO WRITE' over and over again.

I asked Mrs Ball, the school librarian, how I could get over this problem. She said, 'Write what you know.' Well, I am only twelve (*nearly thirteen*), so I haven't exactly had the most riveting of life experiences from which to draw inspiration for a novel. When I told Mrs Ball this, she smiled and then said, 'You have to start somewhere, Skye.'

So that is what I am doing: I am going to have a go at writing about My Mortifying Life.

The trouble is, how do you ever know where the true beginning of a story lies?

In my case, for example, do I start with how Aubrey Stevens has been my best friend since we were three? Because without her, none of this would have happened. She and I have been all but surgically conjoined since the minute we set eyes on each other at nursery.

I can clearly remember that day, even though Mum says it's not possible for me to remember it because I was so small. But I do: Aubrey came toddling over to me while I was playing with one of those shape games where you have to put the cube through the square hole and the pyramid through the triangle hole and so on. I was struggling with the pyramid and Aubrey came right up to me, snatched the shape out of my hand, and stuffed it expertly through the triangle hole. Then she patted me on the head, gave me a slobbery kiss and said, 'Best fwend.'

At least she started as she meant to go on: telling me what to do and how to do it from day one. You can't fault her for consistency. She is as consistent in her bossiness as she is consistent in her always-being-there-ness.

I literally do not know what I would do without her. We go everywhere and do everything together. We even have matching friendship bracelets which we made at a holiday club in Year 5 and which we have sworn we will wear until the end of time. (Or until they fray and drop off of their own accord, which will hopefully be when we are too old and wrinkly to care - but I can't even imagine that.)

Everything about Aubrey is cool. Even her name is cool - way better than mine, but then most names are. I am always telling her that her name is lovely. It makes no difference what I say, though, as Aubrey actually hates it. This just goes to show that people are never happy with what they have.

'I can't *believe* you would want to change your name,' I tell her.

'So would you if your name meant "elf ruler"!' she wails.

She has no idea. I would LOVE it if my dad had chosen my name from the amazing and excellent *Lord of the Rings* trilogy, instead of from a stupid island in the middle of the freezing ocean.

'It could have been worse,' I tell her. 'They could have chosen Galadriel instead. Or Findis.'

Anyway, back to my life, as that is what I am supposed to be writing about . . .

I was apparently conceived (Hideous Word Alert - and equally Hideous Image Alert) on the Isle of Skye in Scotland. So I ended up with the idiotic name, Skye, which I hate with a passion more dark and more fierce than any you can imagine. Actually I hate it just a little less than my APPALLING surname: Green.

'What is so appalling about "Green"?' you may ask.

'Try saying it after my first name,' I may reply.

Yup, that's right, my name is Skye Green. Mum couldn't even get *that* right.

So when people (mainly people like Izzy and Livvy - I'll come to them later) are not calling me 'Skyscraper', or asking me if my head is in the clouds, they are saying, 'Doesn't the sky look GREEN today? Hahahahaha!'

SO HILARIOUS!

Not.

My little brother got the better name, by the way. He is called Harris, also from a holiday in the Hebrides. I guess Scotland did it for Mum and Dad. (Goodness knows why. The only time I have been there I got bitten to death by midges and it rained all the time.)

I did once moan about my name, and Mum said, 'Be grateful for small mercies. We could have called you Eigg or Muck.'

So I guess I am stuck with the name until I am legally allowed to change it.

But anyway, back to my story . . .

Maybe I should start it *right* at the beginning? From when I was a baby?

No, I think not. That would mean I would have to talk about my dad, and seeing as I can't remember him, there's no point in starting there.

He died. That's all you need to know. Don't ask me any more about it, because there's not any more to tell. Mum won't talk about it without blubbing and, like I say, I don't remember. So. I tend to avoid the subject.

Mmm. OK, I'm just going to go for it. I am going to plunge right in and start this story on a typical day in my mad household. After all, I may as well show you *exactly how* mortifying my life is.

You literally could not make it up.

Chapter One

It is the last week of the Easter holidays and I have just about had enough of being at home with my insane excuse for a brother, Harris. At this precise moment in time (i.e. nine o'clock, i.e. breakfast time, seeing as it's the holidays) he is sitting in the dog's bed, checking the dog for fleas.

'Harris, that is gross,' I mutter, flinging my spoon down with a clatter. 'How is anyone supposed to eat around here while you're doing that?'

'It's very important to check Pongo for fleas,' says Harris. 'Especially when he's been snuggling up with Gollum.'

Gollum is our cat. I named her when I was going through a major hobbity phase (encouraged by Aubrey's mum and dad). She hisssssses a lot, so it made ssssenssse, my precioussssssss.

'Harris, since when has Pongo EVER snuggled up with Gollum?' I ask.

My cat is not known to snuggle. She'll share her claws with you, yes. Cuddles? Not so much.

'What are you two talking about?'

Mum has waltzed into the kitchen. Literally waltzed.

'Why are you dancing?' I ask. I take a sip of orange juice and look Mum up and down with narrowed eyes. 'And *what* are you wearing?'

Mum twirls around, holding out a purple satin skirt as though she is about to curtsy. 'You like?' she says, in a silly high-pitched voice. She is also wearing an exceedingly inappropriate clingy low-cut top, covered in silver sequins.

'No! I do not "like",' I splutter. Some of the orange juice goes up my nose.

Harris laughs.

What is it with Mum's dress sense lately? She has taken to going into charity shops and coming out with the most ridiculous collection of lacy, sparkly, velvety, frilly numbers. She calls her new wardrobe 'vintage'. When I told Aubrey that, she laughed and said, '"Vintage" is what old people say when they mean "manky second-hand clothes that other people don't want any more".'

So now I am worried that everyone thinks my mum basically gets her clothes from jumble sales.

'You're not going out dressed like that, are you?' I say.

Mum roars with laughter. 'I should be saying that to *you*, now that you're nearly a teenager.'

I flinch. I hate being reminded that I am nearly thirteen. Ever since Aubrey has turned thirteen she has started doing weird things like stuffing tissues down her bra (which she doesn't even need to wear yet) and talking about boys like they are some fascinating species she has only just discovered, rather than the smelly creeps and lowlifes they actually are.

Mum is still laughing. 'Your *face*!' she says. 'I'm not that much of an embarrassment, am I?'

Harris leaps up from Pongo's bed and yells, 'You're not embarrassing. You're beeeeooooootiful!' and launches himself at Mum's legs. He rugby-tackles her to the floor and they roll around, shrieking and giggling. Pongo loves any kind of rough and tumble, so he joins in.

'For goodness sake!' I shout. 'You are such losers.'

Mum pushes Harris and Pongo off and says, 'That's enough, boys.'

'Aaaaaooooowwwww,' Harris whines. 'But it was fun!'

Mum gets up and gives him one of her indulgent looks as if to say, 'You are such a naughty cutie-pie'. (She has been known to call him this. I have no idea why. Most of the time he is less of a 'cutie-pie' and more of a 'grubby little worm', if you ask me).

'Come on, outside with you,' says Mum.

Harris huffs and puffs but he takes Pongo into the garden and soon they can be heard shouting and barking at each other and doing what only Harris and Pongo do to have fun (which usually involves mud and mess and general nut-headedness).

Mum is looking at me. Her hair is wild and her eye make-up is smudged. She is still panting slightly from the rough-and-tumble. She looks like Roald Dahl's character, Mrs Twit (i.e. quite mad).

'Oh, Skye,' she says sadly. 'It wasn't that long ago that you would have jumped in and joined us. You're growing up so fast.'

'Yeah, well, someone's got to act like a grown-up around here,' I mutter.

Thing is, I wish it wasn't me.

'This'll cheer you up,' Mum says, 'Milly Brockweed tells me that the new people are moving in next door this week.'

'Oh yes, that has brightened up my day no end,' I say. 'Anything to do with Milly Brockweed is bound to be fabulous. Tell me, is it her long-lost son from Australia that she is always banging on about? And will he have a million cats in his house, just like she does?'

Mum sighs. 'Noooo,' she says.

Milly Brockweed is our babysitter and a right old curtain-twitching nosey parker. She also has a houseful of cats which I have to feed when she is away. The first time I agreed to do it, she offered to pay me five pounds. I thought she meant 'five pounds per cat' so of course I was up for it. Turns out she meant 'just five pounds'. Even though I went twice a day for a fortnight and had to put out food all over her horrible house (which smells of cat wee). Gollum made me suffer by being extra-scratchy with me during that time. Can't say I blame her. From her point of view I must have reeked of The Enemy.

'I wish Mrs Robertson hadn't had to move,' I say. Mrs Robertson used to be our babysitter. She lived next door until a few months ago when she had to move into a care home. 'I miss her so much,' I say.

'I know,' says Mum. She puts her arms around me and gives me a quick squeeze. The sequins on her top squash into my face, so I pull away.

Mum releases me and sighs again. 'I miss Mrs Robertson too, but it will be nice to have some new neighbours at last. It's been too quiet with her house standing empty. Maybe they'll be super-friendly and offer to babysit,' she adds, smiling. 'Then I can stop asking Milly.'

'No one can be as nice as Mrs Robertson,' I say, staring at the floor.

Harris and I used to go next door after school when

Mum was late from work. She always gave us homemade cakes and lemonade and helped us with our homework. It's because of her that I love reading so much. When she came to babysit in the evenings, she always read to us. I was a slow learner and not that much good at reading at school, but when I was seven Mrs Robertson read *The Secret Garden* to me and it was like someone had turned on a light bulb in my brain. It is a story about a girl who is sent away to live with a relative she doesn't know or like. She is full of anger until she makes a friend and finds a secret garden which becomes a special place where she can hide. I haven't been sent away from my family, but sometimes I wish I had a special place just for me where I can go when I want to be alone. I suppose that's why I read so much: books are like a secret garden for me.

I asked Mrs Robertson if I could borrow her copy of *The Secret Garden*, and I ended up reading the rest of it on my own and have been a bookworm ever since.

'Well, maybe it will be a nice family with kids your age,' Mum says, breaking into my thoughts. 'Wouldn't you like to make some new friends?'

She is still talking about the house next door.

'New friends?' I say. 'I don't want *new* friends. Why does everyone think that just because I am nearly thirteen I need to grow up and move on and try new things and – and *change* everything?'

Mum takes a step towards me, but I back off. I don't want another faceful of those sequins and Mum's cleavage.

'OK,' says Mum. She looks a bit hurt, but I can't help that.

I open my mouth to say I am going to my room, when Harris bulldozes through the patio doors, a mud-splattered Pongo hot on his heels.

'They're here!' he is shouting. 'The new-people-next-door are here!'

And so begins a new and entirely unwanted chapter in the story of My Mortifying Life.

Chapter Two

The rest of the morning has been taken up with Harris doing his best to find out as much as he can about next door without actually leaping over into their garden and inviting himself in to help them unpack.

OK, so I have been snooping too. In fact, I have been watching out of the bathroom window for . . . let's just say 'a while', as my brother bounces on the trampoline to get a view over the fence. I should really have gone out ages ago and told him that it's easier to see from up here but I can't be bothered. From my higher vantage-point, I can see everything. Not that it has been that riveting. I have watched as the new neighbours (a man and a boy) told the removal men where to put their garden furniture, and I have seen them bring in two bikes, some tools and a lawnmower. So far, so yawn-making.

I wonder if there is a mum as well. If there is, there's been no sign of her.

The man looks nice enough. He laughs a lot as he chats to the removal men. He is tall, has very short brown hair and is wearing dark jeans and a checked shirt. He has a beard – not one of those dirty great bushy ones, thank goodness. I wonder what it would be like to have a dad with a beard. Would it tickle or scratch when he kissed you goodnight? (Why does my brain come up with such weird thoughts?)

I have to lean close to the window to get a really good view. The glass kept clouding with my breath to start with, so I had to wipe it with my sleeve. The boy is almost as tall as his dad. They carried a ping-pong table in just now. They certainly have a lot of stuff. Our garden has the trampoline and a shed full of junk, that's all. We don't even have a table and chairs.

I haven't seen the boy's face properly yet because his straight, black hair falls into his eyes. I wonder how old he is. Well, that has put an end to Mum thinking I would be making a new friend, anyway. There is no way I am making friends with a boy.

Wait a minute: Harris has jumped down from the trampoline and is running inside with an excited grin on his face. I can hear his feet drumming on the stairs. He is probably charging up them two at a time as usual.

I'm going to have to stop: he will tell Mum I was writing in the bathroom and then she will find out about this journal and might even read it. NO!

The door crashes open just as I shove my journal under a pile of towels.

'Hey, watch it!' I cry, as my little brother barges past me to the loo. He starts using it with no consideration of the fact that I am still in the room. 'What are you *doing*?'

Harris looks at me. 'Having a wee,' he says.

'Well next time, don't do it in front of me!' I shout. At least he hasn't asked me what I am doing in here.

Harris pulls a face. Then he says, 'Guess what?

I have been spying on the neighbours. There is a dad and a boy!'

'I know that,' I say.

'Oh.' He looks disappointed.

I watch him go to the sink to wash his hands and the expression on his face makes me feel a tiny bit sorry that I have stolen his thunder. 'So. What exactly have you discovered, Midget Spy 003½ ?' I say, wiggling my eyebrows.

Harris looks up and giggles as he dries his hands. 'One of them plays the drums,' he says. 'I heard them talking about which room they should put them in.'

'And this is good news *how*, exactly?' I ask, as I follow him out of the bathroom and down the stairs.

'It's COOL!' he says, pounding the air with pretend drumsticks.

'What's all the noise?' says Mum, coming out of the kitchen.

'Harris is excited cos next door have *drums*,' I say. 'As if that is something to celebrate.'

'Oh, lovely,' Mum coos. 'Someone with a bit of creativity – that will liven up the street.'

'You won't be saying that when you can't sleep because they're playing the drums all night,' I say.

'Well, I think it's fab,' says Mum.

I cringe. Why does she have to use words like that?

'Yeah!' says Harris, punching the air. 'Maybe they are rock stars.' He starts jumping up and down, holding his arms as though he's got a guitar and begins violently strumming the air.

Mum grabs a hairbrush from the shelf by the stairs. *'Cos we all just wanna be big rock stars!'* she bellows.

'Give me strength,' I say.

'Well, you had better get used to me dressing up in sequins and sashaying along to groovy tunes,' Mum says. She puts the hairbrush back and gives a twirl in the jumble-sale (sorry, *vintage*) satin skirt she showed me the other day.

I stare at her. *'What?'*

Mum beams. 'While you have been spying on the neighbours, I have been Surfing The Net,' she says.

Uh-oh. I scrutinize Mum's face for hints of what to expect next. She is grinning and looking pleased with herself. This does not bode well.

'Have you been shopping online?' Harris asks. 'Oh yay! Have you bought us a new TV?'

Mum ruffles his hair. 'Sorry, little bean,' she says. 'I still haven't won the lottery, so the answer to that will have to be a big fat no.' She makes the kind of noise they play on quiz shows to indicate that a contestant has lost: 'Eeeh-uuuhhh!'

Harris whines. 'Aaaawwwwooo.'

'What then?' I ask. 'Mu-um! Please don't tell me you've been "liking" Aubrey's posts again?'

Mum shakes her head and says, 'No, come into the kitchen and I'll show you . . .'

'Oh my *goodness*!' I cry. 'You haven't gone and posted *another* embarrassing photo of me as a baby so that all my friends can see? Why do you keep *doing* these things?' I drop my head into my hands.

It should be illegal for parents to follow their kids online. Mum is *always* stalking me and posting stupid comments like, 'What are you doing on here? Thought you were doing your homework? ☺ ' When is she going to learn that she is too old for this kind of thing? I can't stand it when she uses 'winky face'. '*Wrinkly* face' would be more appropriate.

'You are ruining my life,' I groan.

'I hate to break it to you, Skye,' says Mum. 'I haven't done any of those things, because – it's a funny thing, I know – but *my* life doesn't revolve one hundred and ten per cent around *you*. In fact,' she says, her eyes glinting, 'for one night a week from now on, it is going to revolve around *me*. Which is what I was about to explain until you got all stressy on me.'

I groan. 'Don't say "stressy". No one says "stressy".'

Mum ignores me. 'Come on, I want to show you the website,' she says, beckoning me and Harris into the kitchen.

'But I want to go back outside and spy on the neighbours,' says Harris.

'You won't have to spy on them for long,' Mum says over her shoulder. 'I'm going to invite them round once they've had a chance to settle in.'

'And once you've had a chance to change your clothes, I hope,' I mutter.

If Mum hears me, she doesn't react. 'So . . .' She goes over to the kitchen table where her laptop is open. 'I have been thinking for a while about getting a new hobby. I was having a look at evening classes—'

'Not this again!' I say. 'The last time you did this we had to listen to you practising Italian all hours of the day and night. *And* you set the satnav to Italian – you nearly crashed the car when you went straight on instead of turning right and ended up on the pavement outside the cinema.'

Mum laughs. 'Oh yes, I'd forgotten about that. *Che scherzo!*' she adds in a sing-song accent.

'Well *I* haven't forgotten,' I say. 'Livvy and Izzy were waiting outside and you almost mowed them down. They have never let me forget it.'

Livvy and Izzy are twins in my year and they are the most evil people I have ever met. Their surname is Vorderman, so Aubrey and I call them the Voldemort Twins, or the VTs for short. They take great delight in the misfortune of others. Particularly in mine.

Mum is rolling her eyes. 'You need to chillax a bit more, Skye,' she says.

'How can I "chillax" and "stop being stressy" when you insist on saying things like "chillax" and "stop being stressy"?' I say. 'Don't forget the time you joined that drawing class and our house was covered in sketches of ugly naked people.'

'That was Art,' Mum says. 'It was a serious life-drawing class where I learned important skills.'

'All those bottoms were very funny,' says Harris, snorting with laughter. He wiggles his own (thankfully not naked) bottom to make a point.

'ANYWAY,' I cut in, before Mum starts going on about the natural beauty of the human body. 'Are you going to tell us what crazy idea you have had for a hobby this time?'

Mum smiles. 'It was this lovely new outfit that gave me the idea,' she said, twirling around.

'Why do you keep doing that?' I ask.

'Because,' she says, curtsying, 'I am going to join a ballroom-dancing class.' She flings her arm out and gestures to the laptop with a flourish.

There on the screen is a site for a class in the town hall. I read it out loud.

'"Tuesday evenings, seven till nine. Learn to dance

together. HAVE FUN! BE STYLISH! GET FIT! Follow in the footsteps of our professionals and you'll soon be tangoing your toes off and waltzing your way to weight-loss!"'

Oh. My. Actual. Life.

Mum has grabbed Harris by the hand and is holding his arm high, spinning him round as though he is a ballerina.

'This is fun. Can I come dancing with you?' Harris says, his eyes shining.

'No, sausage. It's an evening class for grown-ups,' Mum says. She lets Harris go and he makes a big deal out of feeling dizzy, staggering around the kitchen and ending up on top of Pongo, who is snoozing in his basket in a patch of sunlight. (Harris likes joining Pongo in his basket. He does it a lot. That's how weird he is.) Pongo takes this intrusion as a cue for a game: soon the two of them are chasing each other and running rings around the table, knocking the chairs flying as they rocket past.

I feel my stomach go cold as I realize what day it is. 'Tuesday? Did it say Tuesday?' I turn my back on Harris and Pongo and confront Mum. 'It's Tuesday today. You're not going tonight, are you? You can't.'

'Why not?' she says.

'Er, well . . .' I grasp at the first reason that comes to mind. 'School starts tomorrow,' I say.

'Not for me!' says Mum.

'OK, but you should be here for us the night before school starts!' I say.

Mum's face falls. She looks a bit like Pongo when he's been told off for chewing something he shouldn't have. 'I guess so,' she says. 'But I won't be late. I can't miss the first class, Skye.'

For one tiny second I feel my heart go melty at Mum's wounded-puppy face, but then my brain is flooded with images of her doing the foxtrot in spandex and the rumba in sequins – all with other people her age, who no doubt also love spandex and sequins – and all my meltiness hardens into a hot knot of rage.

'You so *can* miss the first class,' I say. 'In fact, you can miss the second and the third and every single one after that!'

Mum looks shocked. 'What has got into you, Skye? What earthly reason have you got for demanding that I give up on this idea? How does it affect you in any way?'

'I'll tell you how,' I say. 'Number one, because it is hideously embarrassing, and number two, because it is the last night of the holidays and there is no way I am putting up with Milly Bad-Breath Brockweed coming round and "babysitting" and telling me I can't watch what I want on TV and that I have to go to bed early.'

'I think ballroom dancing sounds amazing, Mum,'

Harris pipes up, pulling his head out from under Pongo. 'On that show we like watching they are always saying that dancing keeps the elastic bits in your body all elasticky and means you can do awesome stuff like the splits. I can already do the splits,' he adds. He then proceeds to demonstrate while sitting on top of Pongo. 'SEVEN!' he shouts, copying one of the TV show judges. He flings his arms wide in a triumphant gesture.

The dog wriggles with delight and sniffs Harris's bottom.

'Thank you, Harris,' says Mum with feeling. 'At least someone believes in me.' She makes a point of looking at me, her mouth twisting in that way she has when she is trying not to get cross. 'I can see that you don't like being left with Milly, and I am sorry about that, but I don't have anyone else to ask and it will only be once a week. What I can't understand is how you think I will be embarrassing you, Skye? I am hardly going to cha-cha-cha down the High Street in front of everyone we know.'

'You say that now,' I warn her, 'but one whiff of a Latin beat and you will not be able to stop your hips from swinging. That's what they say on that dancing show Harris was going on about. I only watched it once with you and it gave me nightmares. Lots of old, wobbling bodies prancing around to what you call "groovy tunes" while their partners try to heave them up into lifts and spin them around—'

'What a lovely image, Skye,' Mum snaps. 'Anyway, I don't really care what you think – or anyone else, for that matter. I am going to do it. So there.' Her jaw is set at a very stubborn angle. 'In any case,' she adds, 'I need to meet people my own age.'

I gawp at her like a goldfish who has lost all thirty seconds of its memory. '*Meet people?*'

What does she mean by *meet people*? She already knows *people*. She goes to work in an office with 'people of her own age'. Why does she need to meet any more?

'Yes,' says Mum. 'Meet people. As in "make friends".' Her cheeks flush pink as she says this.

Why is she blushing?

Then a huge penny the size of a dinner plate drops into the slot machine of my mind.

Oh no. Oh nonononono. When she says 'people', she doesn't mean *male* 'people', does she? As in *men*? As in *boyfriends*?

I cannot bring myself to ask her this.

I really don't think I want to know the answer.

There is only one person who can help me deal with this.

'I'm calling Aubrey,' I say.

Chapter Three

It is later in the afternoon and the removal men have gone from next door. Aubrey has come round and she and I are sitting on the beanbags in my room. I am hoping and praying that Mum has not rushed around to introduce herself to the neighbours dressed like a giant purple boiled sweet.

Aubrey is putting a lot of concentrated effort into painting her toenails a toxic shade of green. She brought the nail polish with her. I don't have any. I have never seen the point of painting toenails. Most of the time no one gets to see them as they are in shoes or socks or slippers. And who thinks green is a good colour to put on your body anyway? It is the colour of pus.

I have just been filling Aubrey in on Mum's crazy internet-fuelled dreams of becoming the next winner of the *Strictly Ballroom* trophy, but I can tell she is not really listening.

I sigh loudly to get her attention. 'I wish my mum was like yours.'

'Hmm?' she says, finally looking up from her Shrek-coloured toenails.

'I said,' I repeat with a certain amount of impatience, 'I wish my mum was like yours.'

'*What?*' Aubrey scoffs. 'A woman who speaks Elvish and dresses up in long flowing robes to go to HobbitCon to talk to dwarves? Tell you what, I'll swap you.'

You wouldn't think that a household that worships at the altar of all things Tolkien would be a saner place than my home, but let me tell you, it really is.

'At least your mum doesn't prance around in public in low-cut tops and sequins and join a ballroom-dancing class to try and get a boyfriend,' I moan.

'Oh, pur-leeeese,' says Aubrey, rolling her eyes. 'What is so great about my mum?'

'Everything!' I say.

Not that this is what I actually want to talk about, but never mind . . . To be honest, I had expected a bit more of a reaction from Aubrey about Mum wanting to 'meet people' (in other words, find a boyfriend).

I get up and pace the room. 'For a start, your mum doesn't wrestle your brother and dog on the floor and say things like "You've just got to chillax".'

Aubrey snorts with laughter. 'Well, I don't have a brother

or a dog, so that's probably why. And it's a good thing. Imagine what Mum and Dad would have called a boy?'

Aubrey has a sophisticated older sister called Cora who is hardly ever at home. (Sounds like the ideal sibling to me.) She is also named after a character from *The Lord of the Rings*. Aubrey is jealous of her name because 'at least it is normal-sounding'.

I give a dry chuckle. 'Yeah, it might be awkward having a brother called Frodo. Anyway, back to me and *my* life,' I say with emphasis. 'What do you think about Mum's latest crazy idea?'

'So she wants to learn to dance? So what?' Aubrey asks. 'It's not like she's going to pick you up from school in her outfits or anything. Mind you,' Aubrey sniggers, 'do you remember the time she came to get you from swimming dressed as a pirate?'

I hide my face in my hands. 'Don't!' I wail.

'What was that all about again?'

'She had gone trick-or-treating with Harris,' I say, 'and *apparently* "didn't have time to change" before coming to get me.'

'Aw, come on,' says Aubrey. 'It's cool that your mum doesn't care what people think . . .'

'Yeah, like you mean that!' I say.

We both start giggling, as we remember Mum's pirate outfit.

Then something catches my eye out on the street. It is the boy from next door. He is standing on the pavement outside our house, looking up at me. What is he doing? Oh great, he probably thinks I am spying on him now. I turn away and face Aubrey, but she is putting another layer of polish on her toes and has started chatting again.

'. . . and your mum *has* been on her own for a while,' she is saying. 'Maybe it's time she met someone?' She gets up and walks over to the window towards me.

'Why are you walking like that with your toes in the air?' I ask.

'So the nail polish dries properly and doesn't get carpet fluff on it, obviously,' Aubrey replies.

How does she even *know* these things?

'Cheer up, Skye,' she adds as she gives me an awkward hug, leaning forward so her toes don't bash against me.

'Thanks,' I say. 'But Mum has *not* been "on her own". She has me and Harris and Pongo and Gollum.'

'I know,' says Aubrey, releasing me. 'But she *has* been Without A Partner for some time.' She puts her head on one side and smiles.

Why do I get the feeling she is patronizing me?

'Yes, and it's been fine being just the three of us, thank you very much. Why on earth would she suddenly start to talk about *meeting people*?'

'Maybe she's been thinking about this and didn't

want to tell you,' says Aubrey. 'You did say that she's been flirting with Ben from the butcher's counter at the supermarket.'

'I know, I *know*! Don't remind me,' I groan.

I can't go to the supermarket with Mum any more. The moment she sees Ben she puts on this silly, high, girly voice and flicks her hair. (I am sure it is a health-and-safety hazard around all the chops and sausages.) Ben is about thirty, which is obviously ancient, but Mum is at least forty and should know better.

'Oh no,' I gasp. 'What if the flirting with Ben was all training for The Real Thing? What if Mum *meets people* at ballroom dancing and flirts with them and they flirt with her and – Oh! I cannot bear to think about it.'

Aubrey laughs.

'It is not a laughing matter,' I say. Then I add, without thinking, 'Oh flip. I hope Mum doesn't try and flirt with our new neighbour.'

'New neighbour?' says Aubrey. She runs to the window and pushes her face up against the glass. 'You didn't tell me you had a new neighbour.'

'It's not that exciting,' I say. 'Harris was spying on them—'

'WOW!' Aubrey butts in. She jumps away from the window as fast as Gollum did the time she landed on the hob when it was still on.

'What's the matter?'

'Does your new neighbour have a son?' Aubrey breathes.

I frown. 'Yes. At least I think so, I haven't actually met them yet. Why?'

'Is that him out there?' Aubrey nods to the window.

I peer out over her shoulder. The boy is still there, looking up at us.

Flip . . .

'Sit down!' I say, dropping to the floor. I grab Aubrey by the hand and pull her away from the window.

'Ow!' she says, tumbling down on to me. Just before she falls I notice she gives a little wave. 'What did you do that for? You can't wave at him like that!' I say.

'Why not? I was only saying hello,' says Aubrey.

'I don't even know him – YOU don't even know him. It's too weird,' I say.

Aubrey's eyes are shining. 'No it's not – have you seen what a babe he is?'

'A WHAT?' I say.

'A *babe*!' says Aubrey. 'As in "hashtag gorgeous",' she giggles and crosses the first two fingers of each hand over each other.

'Hashtag?' I say. 'Seriously?'

'YEAH! "Hashtag *totally hot*",' Aubrey squeals. 'Look at him! He has the most A-MAZING hair. And those eyes . . . And he looks really cool – his clothes, I mean.' She is literally babbling now.

I don't know what to say. Has my best friend gone as insane as my mum? What is happening to the world as I used to know it?

'So tell me about him,' Aubrey says. She nudges me. 'Stop gawping like a goldfish – you said Harris had been spying on him. What did he find out?'

As if summoned by telepathy, Harris bursts through the door, shoots into my room and launches himself at my bed. 'He plays the drums!' Harris shouts, getting up and bouncing on my bed, which causes the mattress to bow dangerously close to the ground.

'Hey! Were you listening at the door?' I say.

'Of course,' says Harris. 'How else would I know that you were talking about our new neighbours?'

'GET OUT!' I shout.

But Aubrey steps in front of me, eyes shining. 'The drums?' she says. 'Cool! Tell me more, Super Spy Harris.'

Harris giggles. 'I am a cool super spy, aren't I?'

'NO!' I say. 'Do not say another word. And stop wrecking my bed. And GET OUT! Did I not just say that?'

Mum appears in the doorway. Still in her shocking ballroom outfit.

'What's going on?' she asks, hands on hips and trying to look stern. She takes one look at Harris leaping in the air playing imaginary drums, however, and her mouth twitches into a smile. 'Harris . . .' she says, in her hopelessly unimpressive 'telling-off' tone of voice which she reserves especially for him. 'Stop bouncing, sausage.'

'Maybe he's in a band.' Aubrey is still talking about Boy Next Door. 'I wonder if he'll come to our school? How old is he, do you think?'

'Who are you talking about?' Mum asks.

'Excuse me,' I say, squaring up to Mum. 'Will you please leave and take that –' I point to my bouncy brother – 'THING with you?'

Mum sighs. 'Harris,' she says again. 'I get the feeling we are not welcome. Come and help me sort out something for tea – I have to leave for the dancing class at 6.30, so we need to eat early.'

'You are not really going tonight?' I ask.

'Aubrey,' says Mum. 'Don't you think ballroom dancing would be fun?'

'MUM!' I say, before Aubrey can think of a suitable answer. 'Please, just GO!'

Mum shoots me a despairing glance and then grabs Harris by the waist and flings him over her shoulder in a fireman's lift. 'Come on, "Thing Two",' she says to a squealing Harris. '"Let's leave "Thing One" to be grumpy. There's just enough time for a bath before tea.'

Harris protests and kicks his legs, but he is loving every minute of being carried like this.

My insane family leave the room and at last we have peace again.

Aubrey says, 'I wonder if Boy Next Door will join The Electric Warthogs. That would be awesome!'

'The *who*?' I ask.

Aubrey looks as me as though I have just crawled out of a swamp. 'No, not The Who – they are an ancient group of wrinkly old men that my dad likes. Boy, are they lame.' Aubrey gives a dramatic puff and shakes her head to emphasize this point. 'The Electric Warthogs are *way* better.'

'What are you talking about?'

'You *know*,' says Aubrey. 'The band that some of the Year 9s are in. They need a drummer.' She picks up my pencil case from my desk and croons into it. '*I'm just not that into you, yeah, yeah, yeah. Babeeeeee.*'

'What was *that*?' I say.

Aubrey makes an exasperated noise. 'It's one of their songs. Flip, Skye, where have you been since September? They were playing at the school Christmas disco. Oh . . .' She stops herself, her hand flying to her mouth.

A rush of heat fills my head. 'I thought we decided

not to go – in fact, I thought you were ill at the end of last term?' I say.

Aubrey's cheeks have gone pink. 'Yeah. I was. But I sneaked out and went along. Just for half an hour. It was lame. You didn't miss anything.'

I don't know what to say.

She went to the disco without me. But we never go to school discos. Aubrey says they are for losers. So . . . what does this mean?

'Hey,' Aubrey says, her voice false and bright. 'What about if I stay to help you babysit Harris while your mum goes to ballroom dancing? I know you hate that woman Milly What's-'er-face coming round and eating all the custard creams.' Her laugh is shrill and fake too. 'Maybe your mum would let you stay home alone without a babysitter if I was there too? I could call Mum now and ask her if it's OK? I'm sure she won't mind: I am thirteen now after all.'

Yeah, and don't I know it.

I shake my head. 'It's all right,' I say. 'I'm going to tell Mum we don't need Milly any more. After all, I am nearly thirteen too,' I add. There have to be some perks to getting older.

Aubrey's smile fades and her shoulders drop: she looks like an inflatable toy that has had a pin stuck in it. 'Whatever,' she says. She starts to gather her things. 'I

35

had better get going anyway – school tomorrow!'

I walk her down to the hall. Normally I would offer to walk her home, and more often than not, the minute we got to her house, she would offer to walk me back to mine again so that we could carry on nattering. We have been doing this since forever. Our record for walking each other home on one night was twenty-six times.

Not tonight, though. I don't want to risk bumping into Boy Next Door. I open the front door and swiftly check the road for signs of him hanging around. Looks like he's gone.

Goodness knows what Aubrey would actually say to him if she met him – especially now that she has decided he *has* to join our school band. Fingers crossed he won't even be coming to the same school as us.

'So. See you tomorrow then,' I say. 'New term. Boring.'

'Yeah,' says Aubrey. 'Boring as the most boring bore in Boringtown.' She laughs and flicks her hair back over her shoulders. As she does so, I see her glance at next door.

It is pretty obvious that Aubrey thinks this term is going to be the exact opposite of boring. Especially if Boy Next Door has anything to do with it.

Chapter Four

I felt sick with worry once Aubrey had gone. A million and one questions began whizzing around my head, like this:

Why did she lie about going to the school disco? Does Aubrey not want to be my friend any more? Is this why Mum said I should make new friends? Does she know something I don't? Is it something to do with Aubrey turning thirteen and becoming a teenager? Do people dump their life-long friends at this stage in their lives? Is it necessary to completely reinvent yourself?

I mean, I'm not exactly one hundred per cent happy with the way I am, but I am not dead keen on the idea of having to reinvent myself either. What would I reinvent myself as? Although, the way I am feeling right now, I wouldn't mind being able to shapeshift into, say, a cat. Looking at Gollum curled up on my bed, I can safely say I would rather be her than me.

The questions are still swirling even now. It's like I have a tornado in my mind. I am actually feeling quite dizzy. I think I might lie on my bed and stare at the ceiling. I'm sure that's what writers do when they need to sort out problems or search for inspiration . . .

Oh great, now Gollum is lying on my stomach. She is purring loudly, which normally makes me feel happy and safe, but I feel the exact opposite right now. Plus, it is difficult to hold a pen and write straight when you have a cat lying on top of you.

Back to the brain-tornado . . .

Why should turning thirteen change anything? About Aubrey, I mean. It is not changing anything about me, that's for sure. I am nearly thirteen (well, OK, four months to go) and I don't feel any different from how I have always felt. I still love building dens in my room and reading under a duvet by torchlight and pretending I am one of my favourite characters in a book and watching cartoons and . . . basically doing all the things I have always loved doing.

All the things that Aubrey used to love doing with me.

Aubrey and I used to be able to spend a whole day in each other's company talking about stories we'd read and making up new ones. We went through a *Paddington* phase together when we were eight, a *Harry Potter* phase when we were ten and a *Twilight* phase last year. We did endless quizzes along the lines of 'Which Harry Potter character are you?' (I always came out as Hermione, obviously), and we even used to go on some of those FanFic sites and upload our own invented chapters for *Twilight*. (Actually, when I say 'used to', I *might* be still doing it . . .)

We used to pretend that we were Half-bloods and that was why no one understood us. They were all Muggles and had no idea of our special powers. We had secret Harry Potter nicknames for pretty much everyone in our school and spent our break-times plotting what spells we would cast on people we didn't like: hence the Voldemort Twins, Izzy and Livvy.

Aubrey doesn't like doing this any more. She says it is bad enough living in a household full of *Lord of the Rings* nut-heads.

In fact, just the other day she was moaning, 'Books are so last century! Who needs stories when you have YouTube?'

I realize now that I am on my own and, thinking back over the past few months, that Aubrey has not wanted to do the same things as me for a while. Instead she has started reading magazines and blogs and watching vlogs and doing personality quizzes – all stuff linked to celebrity and beauty and fashion and, well, stuff I'm just not that interested in, to be honest. To be fair to Aubrey, she has *tried* to get me excited about the same things as her. She says 'it's really important to know what's hot and what's not'. But I just don't get it.

Talking of what's most definitely *NOT*, Mum has chosen this moment of precious peace and quiet to barge in on my thoughts, calling, 'TEA-TIIIIME!'

I will never write a whole novel at this rate. I bet Jacqueline Wilson never has problems like this to deal with.

Mum bursts into the room. I sit up and take in the scene of horror that stands before me.

'Oh my actual life,' I mutter.

'Ta-DAA!' Mum says, spreading her arms wide and turning round so that I can have the full benefit of the disaster area that is her outfit. She is wearing the silver-sequinned top that is too tight for her and which shows far too much of her cleavage.

Harris appears from somewhere behind the swathes of material that make up the satin skirt.

'Isn't it GORGEOUS?' he breathes.

'Do you like the top, at least?' Mum asks me.

I am lost for words. Luckily Harris isn't.

'I *love* that top,' Harris gushes. 'Can I borrow it for dressing up?'

Give me strength.

'I'm glad *you* like it, little bean,' says Mum. 'This is not going into the dressing-up box yet, though.' She holds out the purple skirt, which seems even swishier than when she first showed it to us, and does another tottery twirl on her shiny high-heeled shoes.

Harris gasps and rushes to take Mum by the hand. She holds his arm up high and lets him pirouette under her, then they both crease up into a fit of red-faced giggles.

'What is *wrong* with you two?' I say.

Harris glares and sticks his tongue out. 'You're just

jealous because Mum looks beautiful,' he says. 'Unlike *you*.'

'Oh yeah, I am soooo jealous of Mum looking like she's about to go to a fancy-dress party,' I say.

Mum beams. 'How funny – I actually did find this top in a fancy-dress shop!' She looks so ridiculously happy that I feel a little bit sorry for her. Surely she doesn't *enjoy* looking through second-hand clothes rails and fancy-dress shops? If we had more money, she would shop in nice places with beautiful things and then maybe she would look like a normal mum. Even Aubrey's mum doesn't go out in public in her *Lord of the Rings* stuff. She saves it for conventions. Also, her outfits are obviously a costume, so people know she is really dressing up as a character. But Mum is always getting this wrong. She thinks it is funny to parade around in weird clothes and that I should 'get a sense of humour'.

'Mum, please at least put a cardigan on before Milly comes round?' I plead.

Not that Milly can comment on what other people wear. She is usually covered in cat hair from her thirteen cats. Pongo always goes crazy when she comes round. It is so embarrassing. Milly, of course, doesn't like Pongo because, as she says, she is 'not a dog person'.

Mum's smile fades and she opens her mouth to speak. Then the phone rings, so she simply shakes her head and goes next door to her bedroom to answer it.

'Oh, hellooooo, Milly!' I hear her say in her talking-to-batty-old-cat-people voice. 'Awwwww. Awwwwww. Really? Awwwwww, noooo! That *is* a shame.'

What's this, I wonder? Sounds as though there's a problem. Most likely a cat-related one, as Milly only ever talks about her cats. But why is she phoning to tell Mum when she was supposed to be coming round here in a bit to 'babysit' me and Harris?

Mum comes back into my room. She is frowning and her face has gone pink. 'That was Milly,' she says.

'Yes,' says Harris. 'We heard you say "Hello, Milly". Then we heard you say "Awwwww" a lot of times. What's wrong?'

Mum sighed. 'She can't babysit because Fluffball, or whatever his name is, has got a poorly tummy so she has to take him to the emergency vet clinic.'

'Oh no!' Harris cries. 'Not Fluffball! He's the white one with the pink nose and the black splodge on his tail.'

'You mean the one that's so fat and so fluffy that he looks like a huge ball of fluff?' I add.

Mum and Harris look at me as though I am the idiot. 'Obviously,' they say in unison.

'So I guess this means I can't go ballroom dancing,' Mum says. She pulls at her swishy skirt and stares down at her shoes.

At this, I feel even more sorry for her than I did when was thinking about her wearing second-hand clothes. She looks likes Cinderella being told she can't go to the ball: she must have been looking forward to this evening more than I had thought.

Then I remember what Aubrey said about babysitting earlier.

'I could babysit instead,' I say, beaming. 'I am nearly thirteen, after all. It's Harris that needs the babysitting, not me. And it's not as if Milly ever does anything when she comes round. She just spends all evening trying to get Gollum to sit on her lap and eats all the best biscuits and tells Harris what a lovely boy he is and makes me go to bed at eight o'clock.'

Mum looks at me with a thoughtful expression. 'Hmm,' she says. 'I don't know, Skye, you are still very young. What if you and Harris started fighting?'

'Of course we won't fight. If you *pay* me to be a responsible babysitter, I will do the job to perfection.' I say.

I watch Mum's mouth twitch into a smile.

Was it cheeky of me to ask to be paid? So what? If you don't ask, you don't get.

'PAY YOU?' Mum explodes into laughter. 'You must be joking!'

Turns out you still don't get, even if you do ask.

'But you would have been paying Milly—!' I begin.

Mum holds up a hand to stop me and I can see that babysitting money slipping through my fingers when . . .

BRRRIIING!

The doorbell goes.

Mum fixes me with a patronizing look and says, 'Looks like I've been saved by the bell. Good try, Skye.'

Chapter Five

Mum goes down to answer the door, her skirt billowing out behind her like a ship in full sail. I can see through the wobbly glass that there are two people standing outside. Which means that two random people are about to see my mum in a too-tight sequinned top and a shiny purple skirt. Which means I wish the ground would open up and swallow me whole.

Mum opens the door, and for a moment she is blocking my view, so all I can see is the top of a man's head.

'Hi,' he says. 'I hope I'm not disturbing anything . . .'

'Oh no!' Mum says. Her voice is high-pitched and ultra-cheery.

No, you're not disturbing us, I think. This is just a regular evening in our looney-tune household.

'Right, er . . .' I can sense the man taking in Mum's outfit. I am torn between wanting to creep up the stairs to see who he is and wishing that I had my own Invisibility

Cloak so that I cannot be seen to be linked to Mum in any shape or form.

Mum gives a little giggle. 'So, do you want to come in?' she asks him.

WHAT? She is asking a strange man into our house and she doesn't CARE that she looks like a bag of recycled wrapping paper?

'Erm, OK,' says the man.

Mum steps back to let him in – and a boy who, it turns out, is standing just slightly behind him.

They are, of course, our new neighbours.

I am sure I see the man look Mum up and down in a surreptitious way as he steps inside. That's it. He thinks she is a weirdo. We haven't even properly met our new neighbours yet, and already they have made up their minds about us.

Mum is wittering on about Pongo, who has rushed out of the kitchen and is trying to shove his nose at the boy in the MOST embarrassing place, and Harris is shouting 'Down, Pongo, down!' and jumping around as much as the dog, which of course makes the dog even more excited. Gollum meanwhile has sensibly retreated upstairs and is hissing at everyone through the banisters. I am tempted to join her.

'So, er, hi!' the man says, edging around Pongo and Harris. 'I'm Rob Parker and this is my son, Finn.

We've just moved in next door—'

'Of *course*!' Mum says, flapping her hands and giggling again. 'I thought I recognized you. Not that I have been spying on you,' she added, which made it sound as though she totally had.

'Skye has!' Harris pipes up. 'I have seen her looking out of the window at you.'

Cheek! He's the one who's been looking over the garden fence.

'Harris,' I hiss. I pinch him on the back.

'Ow! Wha'-you-do-tha'-for?' he whines.

'Stop it, you two,' Mum says, fixing her features into a scary, toothy grin. She laughs again and blushes, then, holding out a hand, says, 'I'm Hellie Green, and this is Skye and Harris. And you've met Pongo!'

Rob shakes Mum's hand.

'Skye Green,' says Finn, and sniggers.

I scowl at him while Mum twitters, 'Oh yes. Ha ha. We didn't really think that one through when we named her, did we?'

'Finn,' says Rob, eyeballing him with a warning look.

Mum has started on my whole life story of how I was named after a Scottish island. She seems to have forgotten about going to ballroom-dancing classes. This would be a good thing if we weren't standing in the hall with two people we don't know, listening to stories about me.

I wonder how far into my life she will get before she thinks of offering anyone a cup of tea. Oh help, I really hope she doesn't offer anyone a cup of tea. At this rate we'll end up spending the rest of the evening listening to the highlights of my life. I have to stop her before she says something really embarrassing.

'Mu-um!' I cut in. 'I don't think they want to know everything about me. Especially not the whole Scottish island thing?' I plead.

The boy sniggers again.

I take a good look at him: now that I am not having to try and get a glimpse from an upstairs window, I may as well see what Aubrey thinks is so 'hot' about him. Also, it is a fact that all writers observe people closely: you never know when you might be able to use something you have noticed in a story. A person's appearance can tell you a lot about them, if you pay attention to detail.

Finn is taller than me. He is standing with his hands in his back pockets in a way that seems to say he thinks he's really cool. He is wearing black skinny jeans and a faded black T-shirt with some kind of band logo on. So maybe Aubrey is right and he will want to be in the school band. Oh please no. Aubrey will go crazy when she finds that out.

I pray that he is *not* going to be coming to our school. Maybe he goes to the school in the next town and he's going to stay there even though he's moved. Maybe his dad is really rich and he goes to some posh place I've never heard of. Maybe – oh boy, Mum has actually mentioned the T-word. Suddenly the prospect of her having to go to ballroom-dancing class is way more inviting than having to spend the evening drinking tea with this boy and his dad.

'Sorry about the chaos, Rob,' Mum is saying as she leads the way into the kitchen. 'The thing is, I was about to go out tonight – to a ballroom-dancing class, hence the outfit,' she says.

WHY did she have to tell him that?

Rob raises his eyebrows and gives a tight smile the way people do when really they are thinking, 'You are a mad person and I need to find a way to escape.'

'In that case, we won't keep you,' Rob says. 'We just thought we should introduce ourselves. We've been a bit tied up getting Finn ready for his new school and so on . . .'

'Oh, there's no need for you to go,' Mum says, taking a step forward and causing Rob to step back on to Pongo. 'I can't go out now, as it happens – our babysitter has let us down.'

Pongo whines and scurries off to his basket.

Rob stumbles as Pongo whisks past. 'Oh, I'm so sorry!' he says.

Finn sniggers again.

Is that the only sound he can make, I wonder? Does he not know how to communicate with his fellow humans?

'Don't worry, Pongo is used to being tripped over,' says Mum, which makes us sound like a family of animal-beaters. 'So, what about that cup of tea?'

'Um, OK,' Rob says.

There is an awkward pause in the conversation while Mum fusses with mugs and tea bags and noisily fills the kettle.

Then Rob says, in a rush, 'I was just thinking, it's a shame about your babysitter. Tell you what,' he says, glancing at his son. 'Finn could hold the fort for you. He's fourteen and he's babysat before, haven't you, mate? I'd be right next door,' he adds, as if this makes it all OK.

Me, babysat by someone only just a year older? Someone my best friend thinks is 'hot'? Someone who sniggers instead of speaking? Someone who is a BOY?

'That won't be necessary,' I say, stepping forward. 'I'm nearly thirteen. I've already offered to babysit Harris.' I fix Rob with a stern look to emphasize *who* exactly is in need of the babysitting around here.

'Oh, well, in that case,' Rob says. 'Looks like you're all set to go out anyway, Hellie. Let's leave these good people to their evening, Finn—'

'Skye, I have told you that you are too young to babysit,' says Mum. 'Sorry,' she adds, turning to Rob. 'We were having a little . . . discussion about this just before you arrived. Skye and Harris do tend to argue, you see. I am not comfortable with them being left unsupervised.'

Rob nods. 'Sometimes it's better to have someone impartial around.' He pauses and looks uncomfortable.

No one seems to know what to say. Please, just leave, I am thinking, when Rob blurts out: 'So, Finn? What do you say?'

'YAY!' Harris shouts, punching the air in triumph. 'We can play Mario together! Skye never wants to play Mario, and Milly never lets me anyway cos she always wants to watch those boring programmes on the telly about knitting and old houses.'

Rob and Mum chuckle.

Nonononono.

This is all getting way out of hand.

I pray that Finn feels as bad about the way things are going as I do. But then Mum goes and utters the magic words – words she refused to say to ME.

'Would five pounds an hour be OK, Finn? It won't be

a late night. I'm only going to the town hall and I'll easily be back by ten.'

I watch in horror as Finn's eyes light up. Then he shrugs and says, 'Guess so.'

Mum's face goes pink with pleasure. 'Thank you so much!' she squeaks. 'I will make you some popcorn quickly before I go. Oh, Rob, you are a lifesaver!' she adds, and leans forward to squeeze his arm.

Rob's face goes pink too, probably from having his arm squeezed by a mad woman in satin and sequins. 'You're welcome. Have a great time at the class. Just throw Finn back over the hedge when you're done with him.'

'Oh, I doubt we'll be learning how to do "lifts" in the first lesson,' says Mum. Then she goes into a completely over-the-top giggling routine as though she has said the most hilarious thing she has ever heard.

Rob's face goes a deeper shade of pink and he lets out a dry chortle. He definitely thinks she's insane now. If only she could keep her mouth shut – the outfit is bad enough, but the lame jokes only add more horror to the situation.

'Yeah, well, you know,' he mumbles. 'Just kick him out when you're ready.'

Harris lets out a ridiculous bellow of a laugh and does a kung-fu kick in the air. 'Hi-yah!' he shouts.

Rob shakes his head and smiles. 'Maybe not quite like that,' he says. Then he reaches out and ruffles Harris's hair and Harris wriggles with pleasure.

Seems like everyone is happy about the evening's arrangements.

Everyone except me.

Chapter Six

Once Rob has gone, Mum hands over the popcorn and asks the kind of question adults always trot out when they can't think of anything better to ask: 'So. Which school are you going to, Finn?'

If they want to find out something about you, why don't adults ask you what your favourite book is, or your favourite food, or your best method of torturing your younger brother? It would tell you a lot more about a person than where they go to school.

'I'm going to start at Westfield Academy tomorrow,' Finn says, taking the bowl. 'Year 9.'

'Oooh!' says Mum, her eyes wide. It's as if Finn has just told her he has invented a recipe for the elixir for everlasting life. 'That's where Skye goes,' she coos. 'You'll be able to introduce him to people, Skye,' she adds, looking extremely pleased with herself.

I curl my lip. 'Yeah. Except I'm in Year 8. I don't suppose Finn will want to meet a bunch of people in the year below him.'

Unless Aubrey has anything to do with it.

Finn gives a lopsided smile and shrugs.

'Well, at least he'll recognize a *friendly face* on his first day,' says Mum. She gives me a pointed look as I scowl back at her.

Do adults undergo some kind of brain surgery when they become parents? I mean, how come they cannot remember how they felt at our age? Or maybe they really are a whole different species and they never felt the way we do. What is there to like about being forced to spend an evening with someone you don't know, and then be told it will be 'nice' that you will recognize each other at school the next day?

Mum is now in Ultra-Hyper Mode as she prepares to leave. She has started issuing a list of instructions at top speed.

'Now, if you need to give me a call, this is my mobile number, only I will have it on "silent" because of course I don't want to disturb the class, but I promise I will check it regularly in case you need to get in touch, but I'm sure you won't as Harris and Skye really are no trouble at all when they are being supervised, and Harris can show you how the TV works and Harris makes the best hot chocolate and if Pongo needs a pee then you just—'

'MUM!' I have to cut in before she dies from not stopping to breathe.

'Yes?' Mum says, panting a little.

'It's fine. You don't need to tell Finn all that stuff. *I'm* here, remember? I don't need to be "supervised". And I know how the TV works and what to do with Pongo and my hot chocolate is pretty good too, thanks very much. So if you are going, why don't you just go? NOW!' I add, as Mum shifts from one foot to the other, looking anxious.

'OK, OK,' Mum says. She sticks a wide grin on her features and says, 'Toodle-oo then! Be good.' Then she leaves. Finally.

Toodle-oo? Since when has Mum ever said 'Toodle-oo'? I glance at Finn to see whether or not this has confirmed his opinion of my mum as a nutter. He has sat down on the sofa and is digging in to the freshly made popcorn. (Rude!)

Harris says, 'Wanna play Mario?'

Finn says, 'Sure.' Then he leans over the back of the sofa and hands Harris the bowl of popcorn saying, 'Your mum's cool.'

'I know!' says Harris. 'So are you.'

He looks at Finn the way Pongo looks at Mum when she is holding a treat above his nose. I half expect my

57

idiot of a brother to start drooling with his tongue lolling out.

I cringe so badly I am worried I have groaned aloud.

Finn laughs. 'Come on, buddy. Let's play,' he says to Harris. 'I warn you though, I am a total legend when it comes to Mario. The heat is on!'

Harris bellows with laughter and says, 'It's way better having a boy babysitter! Can you come every week while Mum is out?'

'Harris,' I growl, 'Finn is not our *babysitter*. He's just come round because Milly can't come tonight.'

'Yeah, DUH! So he's babysitting us instead,' says Harris. He is doing forward rolls over the top of the sofa and on to the floor, running around the back of the sofa and doing it again. And again and again. He is sending the popcorn shooting into the air and all over the floor, and Finn does nothing to stop him, he just laughs.

Then he says, 'Cool! Can I try?'

Before I know what's happening, Finn has leaped over the back of the sofa in one gigantic, long-legged step and is forward-rolling over it as well, landing with a mega-bounce and catapulting the rest of the popcorn into the air.

'Hey!' I shout. 'This is not a trampoline. Harris knows he's not allowed to do this.'

Finn is out of breath from doing manic-monkey

laughing, and Harris is practically peeing his pants with glee.

'We have a trampoline outside!' Harris squeaks. 'Wanna see it?'

Finn grins. 'I know you do,' he says. 'I saw you snooping on us yesterday while you were jumping up and down.' Then he does another forward roll. 'This is way more fun than a trampoline.'

'YAY!' says Harris, copying Finn's every move.

'Both of you, stop it,' I say, scrabbling around on the floor to pick up the popcorn. 'Pongo will sniff this out in no time and eat it all. You *know* popcorn is really bad for him, Harris.'

'"Oooh, you *know* popcorn is really bad for him, Harris",' says Finn in a high-pitched sing-song voice.

Harris shrieks and jumps even higher on the sofa.

I growl and turn to leave the idiot boys to it and am almost flattened by Pongo, who has burst through from the kitchen exactly on cue – he must have heard his name or smelt the popcorn. He immediately begins scoffing as many pieces as he can while I shout at Finn to hold him back. Both boys are completely useless with laughter by now. They are rolling around on the sofa like a pair of puppies themselves, squashing popcorn into the fabric and making even more of a mess.

Suddenly I wonder why I am bothering trying to get

them to calm down. It is not *me* making the mess and it will certainly not be *me* clearing up Pongo's poo or sick or whatever he does as a result of eating the popcorn.

I get up off the floor and brush the crumbs off my jeans. 'Fine,' I say. 'If you two want to behave like animals, you can deal with *that* animal when it all goes wrong.' I point at Pongo who has turned into a canine Hoover, his face pushed as flat to the floor as he can, so that he can get as much popcorn into his mouth as quickly as possible. 'I am going upstairs,' I say.

'OoOOOOooo!' says Finn. 'She's going *upstairs*. I'm scared, Harris – what about you?'

Harris is squealing like a piglet now. He is bright red in the face and has reached that point of over-excitement I like to think of as 'danger-point', which basically means that Pongo might not be the only one having an accident of some sort this evening.

I smile to myself. Finn will just have to find that one out for himself, won't he? After all, he is being paid to *babysit*.

I leave the two boys and the dog wrestling in the sitting room and go up to my room to read. I think about texting Aubrey to tell her what a nightmare I am having, but then I think again: she might invite herself round if I mention Finn is here.

No-way-José am I going to introduce Finn to Aubrey.

It is bad enough that he has ganged up on me with my own brother. There is no chance in a million years that I am going to let him come between me and my best friend as well.

Chapter Seven

I woke up this morning with a sense of dread sitting heavily on my chest. It took my sleep-logged brain a while to crank into action. I couldn't think what was making me feel like that. I made a huge effort to open my eyes and try to shift and stretch.

Then I realized the heaviness was actually caused by Gollum, who was sitting on me in her favourite position, her face pushed into mine. She was purring loudly and drooling on my neck. She is my own personal furry (and dribbly) alarm clock.

She hissed when I complained. Now she is miaowing loudly, making it clear I am supposed to be up and getting her breakfast.

Well, tough, Gollum. I can see by the clock next to my bed that it is still only 6.30, so you'll have to wait.

Hang on a minute. I have just remem
what day it is: the first day of a new term.
And the first day of going to school with my new
next-door neighbour, who is an A-grade annoying
boy, but who my best friend thinks is a 'hashtag
gorgeous babe'.

I can feel the heaviness in my chest returning
as I write, and this time it has nothing to do
with Gollum.

I'm going to have to get up and face the
day sometime, I suppose. Maybe it won't be
that bad after all. Maybe I am worrying over
nothing. Maybe . . .

I follow my cat downstairs. On the way into the kitchen
I pick up my mobile which I left on charge last night.

I think back to Mum coming home from her
dancing class. She was irritatingly happy. Even the
fact that Finn was vacuuming the sofa did not stop her
from grinning. You would think that seeing a teenage
boy using a Hoover would ring some alarm bells, but
she just beamed and asked him what had happened.
He said that *I* had given Pongo some popcorn and
that it had made a mess, but that Mum didn't need

to worry, because he had cleared it all up now. Mum then thanked him for being so thoughtful and handed him a wad of banknotes! She wouldn't listen when I told her I had nothing to do with the mess. If only she had seen the state of the place five minutes earlier: furniture rearranged into an obstacle course, popcorn squashed into the cushions, and dog-sick on the carpet.

If I hadn't felt so outraged, I would have felt admiration for the amazing job Finn did at hiding the evidence. However, my blood was almost literally boiling after the comment about Pongo. How could he drop me in it? It was bad enough that Harris had made him into some kind of hero. Not only is Finn turning my own family against me, he is prepared to tell lies about me as well.

I feel all the anger from last night surge through me again as I scrape some cat food out of the tin and into Gollum's bowl. Then I take my phone with me into the garden as I let Pongo out for his morning pee. Maybe I should text Aubrey to warn her what Finn is really like.

Aubrey has beaten me to it – and boy, has she been busy! She has sent not just one text, but hundreds. I smile as I scroll back through them. What have I been worrying about? I went to bed last night almost convinced she would be dumping me today at school. There is nothing wrong between us, I think, as I see how many times she has texted: this is the Aubrey I know and love. I will tell her about Finn and everything will be OK. She will see my side of the story. She is the only person in the world who truly understands me.

I feel guilty as I realize I should have checked my phone last night while Finn was here. Maybe I should even have texted her to tell her right there and then what a loser he is. She will think I have been blanking her now.

I feel less guilty as I scroll back and read all the texts from the beginning, though: most contain questions about the new neighbours rather than any worries about why I haven't texted back. They pretty much all look something like this:

Have U seen Mystery Boy again? 😊

Have U MET Mystery Boy? 😶

R U with him now? WELL JELL IF U R! 😊

I can't help smiling at this one, though, as I can almost hear Aubrey saying it.

Suddenly there is an almighty crash from next door. I jump, startled, and nearly trip over Pongo who is excited by the racket and is hurtling around me in circles.

'What was—?'

A volley of thuds fills the air: it sounds as though a

giant is falling down the stairs. This is swiftly followed by another crash.

Pongo whines and rushes back into the house.

I follow him.

Mum is making a cup of coffee.

'Did you hear that?' I ask, pointing back into the garden.

'Hmm?' says Mum, sleepily.

Harris hurtles through the door. 'Finn is practising his drums! I can hear it through the wall. It's awesome!' He pulls two wooden spoons from the utensils pot on the work surface and starts drumming the tabletop.

'HARRIS!' I yell.

'You two,' Mum groans. 'Not now.'

'Huh! It's not me using the table as a drum kit!' I protest.

Mum takes the spoons from Harris and tells him to sit down.

I grit my teeth and look back at the frenzied messages from Aubrey.

'So, Finn seems like a lovely boy,' Mum says. 'Put your phone down, Skye.'

'Lovely? More like Draco Malfoy's uglier and more evil cousin,' I mutter.

'He is COOL and AWESOME and AMAAAZING!' says Harris, bouncing up and down in his chair.

I give him a Paddington-style hard stare.

'What did you guys do last night?' Mum asks. 'I never asked. I said put your phone down, Skye,' she adds, without pausing for breath.

Of course you didn't ask! You weren't thinking about us. Your head was in the clouds after a night of waltzing around 'meeting people', I say. In my head. I slam my phone down, grab the cereal, pick up a spoon and then scowl for good measure.

'Thank you, Skye. Welcome to the Land of the Living,' says Mum.

She thinks she is so funny.

I open my mouth to speak but Harris is already talking.

'We played Mario and we ate popcorn,' he says, doing his best impression of the well-behaved child that he NEVER is.

Mum's smile broadens. 'Sounds a lot nicer than an evening with Milly,' she says. 'So you won't mind if I ask him to come again next week?'

I drop my spoon into my cereal bowl with a clatter. 'WHAT?'

'That's one way to get your attention,' says Mum.

'I am NOT having him round again,' I say.

'It's Finn or Milly, young lady,' Mum says, fixing me with her Don't-mess-with-me expression.

I realize Mum must be serious about this latest hobby. 'So you are going *back* to the ballroom-dancing class?' I ask, horrified.

'You betcha,' says Mum. She clicks her fingers and waggles her hand down in front of her in what she clearly thinks is a smooth move.

'Don't do that,' I groan.

Mum's smile fades and she sighs. 'I had a lot of fun last night, thanks for asking, Skye,' she says. 'And it did me good to get out and meet people.'

There she goes again with the whole 'meeting people' thing. I narrow my eyes.

'What "people" did you meet exactly?' I ask.

'*Dancing* people of course, stupid!' says Harris, flicking a spoonful of wet Cheerios at me.

'Shut *up*!' I shout. I push my chair back and make a lunge for him, but he is too fast. He bounds from his chair and leaps through the air, then grabs a tea towel from the work surface and begins spinning it around his head. 'Did you do this dance, Mum?' he asks, giggling. 'It's called the Tangfastic.'

Mum laughs. 'Actually it's the tango,' she corrects him. 'And no, we didn't – it's a very difficult dance. Don't forget, I'm a beginner.'

'But you will learn the tango, won't you?' Harris asks, dropping the tea towel on Pongo's head.

The dog shakes it off and then begins another one of his Let's-chase-Harris games, yapping and jumping and fake-snarling.

As Obi-Wan Kenobi once said, 'Who's the more foolish: the fool, or the fool who follows him?'

Mum ignores them.

'I don't know about the tango,' says Mum. 'I tell you what I *am* going to do, though. I am going to enter the end-of-term competition and then maybe you can come and watch me – if it doesn't finish too late, that is?'

'No WAY,' I say. I have totally had enough of this insanity. I hear my phone ping and see that Aubrey has texted yet again. 'I am going now,' I say.

'Don't you want a lift?' says Mum.

I look at her chosen outfit of the day: a fake red flower in her hair, a red jumper with a feathery scoop neckline, and long wide-legged black trousers with embroidered red flowers on, all finished off with red shiny DMs. 'Er, no, you're all right,' I say. 'I'll get the bus.'

I walk out of the house to the sound of Harris wittering about how he wants to enter the dance competition too and how he's going to help Mum with her outfits and practising her dance.

As Aubrey might say: 'I think they need to go to the Life Shop.'

I glance at her most recent text as I walk to the bus stop:

> R U dead or something? LOL. 😊

I sigh and text back:

> Still alive. Trying to ignore Boy Next Door and brother. Been on Planet Hunger Games since last night. Kidnapped by Katniss 🐱

It's a lie of course. I read all those books years ago. But it was the first thing that popped into my head.

The bus pulls up as a little thought bubble appears on the screen which means that Aubrey is reading my text. She's either writing a really long response or she's thinking hard about what to say.

I get on the bus waiting for her to answer. Once I have found a seat I check my phone again.

> Tell me ALL about it. C U L8r. Mum is giving me a lift today. Going out with Dad. She is Galadriel. Dad is one of dwarves. Kill me now. 😟

I grin as I text back. Aubrey is back on form. I can tell her everything and things will be OK.

Chapter Eight

I walk through the school gates and immediately spot Aubrey standing by the netball courts. She sees me and waves. I feel a fizz of happiness. Skye and Aubrey – Aubrey and Skye: Best Friends Forever (BFF, as we used to say).

'Hey!' she calls as I make my way towards her. 'I was beginning to worry that you'd been swallowed up by a wormhole and spirited away into a parallel universe or something.'

I grin, feeling sheepish. 'Yeah, sorry – you know what I'm like when I'm in book-hermit-mode. I just kind of hibernated last night. Wasn't looking forward to coming back to this place for starters.'

Aubrey threads one arm through mine. ''S'OK. Talking of "modes": Mum was in super-organizational-mode last night, making me pack my school bag under her prison-guard-style supervision. AND – get this – she told me I have a *dentist* appointment after school today!' She makes a disgusted noise. 'I HATE my dentist. He has the hairiest nose you've ever seen. "Hashtag GROSS"!'

'Eeuw!'

'I know. And there's no way I can avoid looking up it while he is staring into my mouth,' she goes on.

This is a game we sometimes play – seeing who can gross the other one out the most. The bell goes and we shriek and giggle and think up things that are even more disgusting than Aubrey's dentist's hairy nostrils as we follow the hordes into the building. We are walking down the Year 8 corridor, completely unaware of anyone else around us as we laugh and joke. I am feeling fantastic.

Until I hear someone come up behind us and say, 'Hey, Orrrbreeeee-and-Skye,' in a sneery voice.

It is Izzy, one half of the Voldemort Twins.

Aubrey whirls round and squares up to them. Her expression hardens and I think she must be about to tell her to get lost, but instead she says, 'Oh, hey, Izzy. Whassup?'

Whassup? This is Izzy Voldemort she is talking to. We do not say 'Whassup?' to Izzy Voldemort.

I am about to pull Aubrey away and ask her what the flip she thinks she is doing when Izzy steps closer to me, ignoring Aubrey, and says, 'So how were the holidays, Hermione? Play much Quidditch, did you?' She simpers.

'Or were you too busy *reading* and being a general all-out *nerd*?' She shoots me a nasty, slit-eyed, snaky smile. 'We missed you at the cinema last week, didn't we, Aubrey?'

There is a cackle as Livvy appears at her side (no doubt by some kind of evil Summoning Charm).

'Looks like you guys had an awesome holiday,' says Aubrey, letting go of my arm. I swear she even gives me a little shove out the way.

'What was that about the cinema?' I want to ask Aubrey, but I can't form the words. I watch in horror as she flicks her hair and mirrors the twins' body language: hands on hips, superior smile on lips. What is she doing?

'I saw the pictures you posted, Livvy,' she goes on. 'Good times.'

'Yeah, I noticed you stalking me,' says Livvy, her smile turning sour enough to curdle milk. 'You "liked" every single thing I posted – even the photo of the display board at the airport showing how delayed our return flight was.'

'Yeah. Not very *supportive*,' says Izzy. 'Surprised you have time to look at our posts. Weren't you too busy playing make-believe games and writing *stories* with your little chum here?' she adds, nodding to me.

Aubrey opens her mouth to respond, but the Voldemort Twins cackle in unison and link arms, turning to go. They always have to have the last word. Part of me is relieved that they are being mean: I must have misread Aubrey's body language just now.

'Leave it, Aubrey,' I say, laying a hand on her arm. 'You know what they are like.'

Aubrey nods and blinks hard. 'Let's go,' she says.

I can see she is upset. Those twins are such stirrers. Why did they even say that thing about the cinema? A nagging little voice in my head reminds me that Aubrey did go to the disco without me. Maybe she went to the cinema without me too?

No, the VTs were just winding me up. As usual. Aubrey would never hang out with the Voldemort Twins. I link arms firmly with my best friend and we head to our lockers.

The atmosphere between us is a lot less relaxed as we start unpacking our bags. I am trying to think of something to say to cheer Aubrey up when I see my locker door. Oh great. Someone has kindly Tippexed 'Skye Diver' all over it. I touch the white letters – still wet. No prizes for guessing who did this. I look around for the Voldemort Twins, but they have clearly used the Dark Arts to transport themselves elsewhere.

I am about to say something about it to Aubrey when she starts talking first.

'So,' she says, unloading the contents of her school bag. 'You were going to tell me all about last night. You said something about "avoiding Boy Next Door"? What happened?'

I really don't want to talk about this now. I just want us to get back to normal. 'Oh, nothing,' I say. 'I told you – I was in my room all evening.'

Aubrey looks at me. I know she can tell just from my tone of voice that I am hiding something. We have always been able to read each other like a book.

'Anyway, I have to talk to you about Mum,' I say, clutching at a change of subject. 'I am seriously worried. She says she's going to enter a dance *competition* and that it was "nice meeting people" last night—'

'Hmm,' says Aubrey. 'So when are you going to introduce me to Hot Neighbour Boy? Have you found out his name yet, by the way?'

She is not paying attention to me. She is not even looking at me now. She is aligning her books in her locker with great concentration. Honestly, she complains that her mum goes into super-organizational-mode, but I have to say it is getting to be a serious case of 'like mother like daughter'. What does she think she is doing? Oh my life: she is colour-coding her stationery! OCD, or what?

I have to stop her right now, as I can tell from the look of concentration on her face that otherwise I will not get her full attention until she has finished. I decide I am going to have to tell her exactly what Finn is like. I will tell her how he lied to Mum about me giving Pongo popcorn and making him sick. That way she will see how mean he is and she'll lose interest in me 'introducing' them.

'Sure. I'll tell you *all* about Boy Next Door,' I say.

Aubrey immediately stops fiddling with her locker and turns to face me, eyes shining. 'Go on!' she says.

Gotcha.

I take a deep breath. 'So. First of all, Mum asks him – he's called Finn by the way – to BABYSIT us. Can you believe it? Milly Badbreath couldn't make it, and just as I am about to convince Mum that Harris and me would be OK home alone, Finn's dad, Rob, rings the doorbell and ends up volunteering his son to stay and "look after" us. And Mum only stands and chats to him in her *hideous* sequins-and-spandex outfit as if everything is normal and then she leaves us with Finn and it is a *nightmare . . .*' I tail off.

Aubrey has lost interest. It is because I started talking about Mum instead of giving her gossip about Finn. She is tutting over the fact that a protractor has found its way into the pen compartment in her oversized pencil case.

'Aubrey?' I say.

Aubrey puts the pencil case down and turns, putting her hands on her hips again. 'What?' she asks.

'Mum is determined to ruin my life,' I say.

Aubrey rolls her eyes. 'Oh come on. Your mum is lovely! Anyway, I thought we were talking about Finn.'

I groan. 'I was, and now I am talking about Mum. She is a nutter!'

Aubrey giggles. 'Don't be mean. Anyway –' she leans in conspiratorially. 'Back to more important matters: how come you didn't text me the *minute* Finn otherwise-known-as Hot Boy Next Door came round last night? Is this all a plan to keep him to yourself?' She does a weird kind of nudge-nudge-wink-wink manoeuvre, which I am guessing is supposed to mean that I too think Finn is 'hot'.

I open my mouth to deny this, to apologize for not texting, to elaborate on the Pongo-and-popcorn story – anything to stop her looking at me like that and speaking in that frankly rather sick-making tone of voice – when Aubrey lets out a gasp and drops the book she is holding. On my foot.

'OW!' I say, hopping up and down.

'Shh!' says Aubrey. She flaps her hands at me and shrinks back against her locker. I realize she is staring at a point past my right shoulder.

I stop hopping and turn to follow her gaze. I can't see anything worth gawping at. I turn back to face her, frowning.

'Aubrey? What . . . ?'

My friend looks odd. Her face has gone shiny, as though she is bathed in golden light from on high. She looks literally awestruck.

Then she breaks out of her statue-mode and flicks her hair, dips her head and smiles in a shy kind of way while blinking as though she has got something in her eye. When did this whole hair-flicking thing start? She never used to do it. She looks as though she is having some kind of fit.

'Are you feeling OK?' I ask.

'Shh,' she hisses again through her fixed smile. 'It's him!'

I turn slowly back again.

No. Nononononono. The reason for Aubrey's bizarre behaviour is standing by the Year 9 lockers.

It is, of course, Finn. He looks a bit lost. A tiny part of my brain tells me I should go and say hi, but then my sane brain clicks in and reminds me that Finn Parker is my nemesis. *And* he is my best friend's heart's desire. I look back at Aubrey who is clutching a folder to her chest and grinning at Finn as though she has fallen into a hypnotic trance. Any minute now she is going to do her own impression of the *Romeo and Juliet* 'Wherefore art thou?' scene. This is enough to stop me from feeling even a weensy bit sorry for him being a newbie.

I try to think of something to distract Aubrey and get

us away from Finn, but my mind has gone blank.

'He is *seriously* hot,' Aubrey whispers. 'Even better than from a distance. Look at those eyes! Like . . . like almonds!'

'Like *what*?'

'And that hair! Is his dad Asian? He's sooooo beautiful . . . He even makes school uniform look cool. Capital O. Capital M. Capital G!' she breathes. 'You *have* to introduce me this minute.' And she gives him a girly little wave with her fingers and giggles like a half-brained moron. Luckily Finn has not noticed Aubrey and now one of the Year 9 boys is talking to him.

'Come on,' I say. 'Let's go to the form room.'

'Say hi,' she says quietly. 'Go and get him to come over!'

'You get him to come over if you're that bothered,' I say.

'I can't!' Aubrey says. Her face collapses and her shoulders sag as if she is in severe pain.

Flip. It's like she's possessed. I think of all the sci-fi stories I have read, where aliens come and wipe your memory clean and you wake up with a different personality. If I didn't know differently I would think this is what has happened to my best friend. I no longer recognize her.

She is fluttering her eyelashes now and trying to get

into Finn's line of vision again.

I am speechless for at least one whole minute as I stand there and watch Aubrey making a complete fool of herself. Then I snap into life and grab her wiggly-fingered hand and force her to look me in the eye.

'He's mental!' I say in a low voice. 'I keep trying to tell you. He spent the entire evening rolling around on the floor with Harris and Pongo and squashing popcorn into the carpet. That is why I didn't text you – because there was *nothing interesting to tell*.'

Aubrey's expression darkens. 'You could have invited me round,' she says.

I let out an exasperated sigh. 'You are not listening to me, are you?' I glance over my shoulder. It is my turn to gasp now – but in mortification, not luuurve. 'He's looking at us,' I say. I keep my eyes fixed on Aubrey and lower my head so that my messy hair falls across my face to hide it from Finn.

'Is he?' Aubrey squeals. 'I'm going to literally die!' she says. She flaps her hand in front of her face as though to fan herself and giggles like a demented monkey.

'Aubrey, you are not going to *literally* die. It would make a nasty mess and cause complications for the school nurse.'

She doesn't react. She just carries on gawping at Finn.

'Listen to me,' I insist. I try to stand in her line of

vision. 'Finn is really *not* a nice guy. OK? He completely ignored me and made a massive mess in our house and when Mum came back she asked him what had happened and he said it was my fault. And Mum believed him AND she paid him fifteen quid AND she asked him to come again next week!'

At that point the bell rings and everyone starts scurrying past us to get back to lessons.

'Next week?' says Aubrey, as people push and jostle us. 'In that case, if you won't introduce me, I'll have to come round to help babysit next week – just try and stop me!'

Chapter Nine

School is a living hell for the rest of the day. I find myself actually missing the days when all I had to worry about was a bit of cattiness from the twins. That was a picnic with fairy cakes and ice cream compared with Aubrey going on and on about Finn.

Any chance she gets during the day she is talking about him, dreaming about what it will be like to talk to him, pondering about where he comes from and what he is into. She even gets hold of a magazine at break and consults it as though it is an Oracle of Luuurve.

'It says here,' she says, flicking through *Teen Girl*, 'that you have to play it cool if you want to get the guy of your dreams. Maybe that's where I am going wrong?' She looks up at me, her forehead crinkling.

'Can't see how that's going to work,' I mutter. 'He hasn't noticed you when you wave at him, so how is he going to notice you if you play it cool? Why don't you just go up and say hi and get it over with?'

'But that's the whole point,' says Aubrey. 'If he hasn't noticed me when I am being totally obvious, then I have to use "reverse psychology",' she says with emphasis, stabbing her finger at the page. 'Then he might "realize what he is missing",' she adds. 'It says, "If you love someone, let them go—"'

'Oh yeah, let me guess,' I cut in. ' "If they come back, it means nobody else liked them, so you'd better set them free again".' I snigger.

Aubrey frowns. 'No, it doesn't say that,' she says. 'It says "If they come back, they are yours".'

I let out a heavy sigh. I don't know why I bother saying anything. Even my sarcasm is lost on her now she is in über-loved-up-mode.

Thankfully Aubrey doesn't get another chance to catch sight of Finn. The first day back at school is always pretty hectic with endless assemblies and lessons on how to write your name in your new books and how to walk sensibly when crossing the road for the bus.

I finally get a reprieve from her love-struck wittering at the end of the day when she goes to get the bus into town to go to the dentist. (I do wonder why she didn't go in the holidays, but at the same time I am glad she is busy and can't try and invite herself over to spy on Finn.)

I get on the bus going in the opposite direction from Aubrey and decide not to turn my phone on, just in case she bombards me with Finn-related questions all the way to the dentist's waiting room.

It is a lovely peaceful journey during which I manage to dream up some pretty cool descriptions of the VTs with their crocodile-smile faces. On the short walk from the bus stop to my house, I start planning what I am going to do later once I've finished my homework when I realize that someone is walking behind me.

I keep my head down and pray it isn't Finn.

'Hey.'

It is Finn.

I half turn my head, keeping my face shielded by my scruffy hair. 'Hey,' I mutter.

'D'you always get the bus?' he says. He takes a couple of longer strides to catch up with me.

I glance sideways at him. 'Depends.'

Finn nods. He hoists his bag higher up on to his shoulder.

We walk along in silence. I cannot believe he is getting the bus too. Am I going to have him in my face everywhere I go from now on? Wait till Aubrey finds out. She is going to love it . . . This is horrendous.

I try to keep a pace ahead of Finn, but it's tough as he's so much taller than I am. I wish he would either fall back or run ahead, as I can't think of anything to say to him other than 'Go away', but I can't quite bring myself to say that. I actually don't want to be drawn into any kind of conversation, even one that shows Finn just how much I resent him.

We have reached our houses. I look up at them. They are joined together. Not all the houses on our street are like this. Some of them stand alone. Suddenly, seeing our houses joined like this, it feels like an ominous sign: Finn moving in on my life, pushing into my space. For the second time that day I find myself wishing I possess some kind of magical power. I would so love to be able to split the houses in two and banish Finn and Rob as far away from us as possible. Or bring Mrs Robertson back. That would be the best thing I could do.

I open our gate, taking care not to look at Finn.

'So, maybe see you tomorrow?' he says.

I jerk my head up. I feel the blood drain from my cheeks. There is no *way* I am going to let him anywhere near me at school. Aubrey would pounce on him like Gollum hunting a mouse. Although with less hissing and blood and guts involved. Tempting as that image is, I shake my head to banish it immediately because Finn is looking at me strangely. I hope he can't read my mind. That is the only place where I am safe from him.

'Sure,' I say, then I get my key out and fumble with the lock.

'See ya, then,' he says, as he lets himself in through his door.

Not if I see you first, I think.

Chapter Ten

GAH! Turns out I didn't get a chance to see him first . . .

DOUBLE GAH!!

Today is going to be the most humiliating day of my life. How do I know this? Because I am sitting in the car *next to Finn* on my way to school.

I KNOW! I never get a lift to school, so I should be pleased. But (a) I am being driven by Mum, who is wearing possibly the most insane outfit ever seen on another human being in real life (more on that later); and (b) I am sitting NEXT TO FINN.

If Aubrey sees us arrive together I will be dead on so many levels I may as well start planning my funeral right now. She texted me last night asking me AGAIN when I was going to introduce her to Finn. I avoided the subject. I am not going to be able to avoid it when I arrive at school with him BY MY SIDE, am I?

Aubrey also sent me another text before signing off which was a bit bizarre. It said:

> Had a gr8 time this afternoon! C U 2moro! 👍😄

When I texted back -

> What do U mean? Did you have a gr8 time at the dentist, you freak?! 😿

- she replied:

> Oh yeah! 😵 Meant it was gr8 to be back at skool wiv U 😺 Looking 4ward to seeing you tomoz xxxx

I was puzzled and thought my best friend was being a bit needy. But hey, at least my thoughts about us growing apart were probably not justified. So I was looking forward to seeing her too.

UNTIL NOW!

Let me backtrack to explain . . .

The day started at 6.30 a.m. with hooting and shrieking and the most appalling music coming from the kitchen, which is right underneath my room. At least it meant that Gollum was not sitting on me, suffocating me again. She was as shocked as I was by the racket coming from downstairs and had taken refuge on top of my wardrobe.

I shuffled down to breakfast, my face heavy with sleep, to find Mum, Harris and Pongo spinning round and round while Harris twirled something above his head and made loud whooping noises.

I walked over to the radio and turned the music off. Harris whined and immediately raced over to switch the radio back on again. I put my hand out and pushed it against his forehead to stop him running into me.

Then we were rolling on the floor, fighting and screaming at each other and Pongo was joining in, wagging his tail and licking my face.

So far, so normal.

Mum, of course, did nothing to stop any of this. She merely raised her eyebrows, took a sip of her coffee and said, 'Oh dear, someone's got out of the wrong side of bed this morning.'

Coming from the woman who looked as though she had fallen into the *clothes recycling bin outside the supermarket!* She was wearing a lime-green satin dress with black lacy trim. And dancing to ear-injuring 1980s power ballads with her eight-year-old son and a dog.

At breakfast! On a weekday! What if the postman came and rang the doorbell? What if one of the neighbours popped by? Then she would be seen IN PUBLIC like this.

She thought I had got out of bed the wrong side? I say she gets out the wrong side every day and smacks her head against the wall. It is the only way to explain her complete and utter inability to behave like a normal human.

Then, just to put the icing of disaster on my cake of doom, the doorbell DID have to ring, didn't it? And guess who it was?

Finn and Rob.

For one moment I had hoped they were coming to complain about the rumpus Mum and Harris had been making, but no. They wanted to remind us that the bus wasn't running this morning because of the roadworks in town, so could Mum possibly give Finn a lift to school with me because Rob had just been called to an urgent meeting and had to leave early. They had heard the music and assumed we would be up. (So the music really was that loud. The shame!)

From the look on Rob's face, he hadn't assumed that Mum would be practising the salsa wearing a dress which looked like a nuclear-reactive bin-bag.

And from the look on Finn's face, he was loving every second of my very obvious mortification.

At least I am not having to speak to him on the way into school: he has plugged himself into his headphones and turned his back on me. I don't blame him. Mum and Harris have put the radio on and are singing along to 'Bohemian Rhapsody' at top volume. Harris is doing the 'Galileo' part at a pitch that will soon have all the neighbourhood dogs chasing our car if he doesn't tone it down a bit.

I know I say I don't much want to change and grow up and stuff, but sometimes I wouldn't

★ ★ ★ ★ ★ ★ ★ ★ ★ ★ ★ ★ ★ ★

mind being able to leave home.

Oh no, we've pulled up in the car park at school and I can see Aubrey and the VTs are walking in together, heading towards the locker area already. Hide me, someone, PLEASE!

★ ★ ★ ★ ★ ★ ★ ★ ★ ★ ★ ★ ★ ★

Chapter Eleven

Finn gets out of the car as soon as Mum pulls up at the railings and mumbles, 'Thank you, Mrs Green.' Then he slouches off, headphones still on, head down, shoulders hunched.

'Aww,' says Mum, watching him go. '"Mrs Green"! Isn't that cute?'

'Pur-leeeze!' I mutter. I am impressed with Finn's quick getaway, though, so I attempt the same technique, but I am fumbling too much with my notebook and school bag. I don't get more than three paces away from the car before Mum has wound down the window and is calling after me.

'Skye, darling!' she wheedles. 'Don't I even get a kiss?'

I freeze as the group of people in front of me turns to see who's shouted those cringe-making words. I keep my back resolutely turned on Mum and fix my eyes on the ground, hoping she'll get the message, shut up and drive off.

However, as I see expressions on the faces of the people in front of me change from mild interest into full-on glee and amusement, I hear Harris yell:

'Skye! Skye! I can see your knickers – your skirt is tucked into them!'

Mum decides it is time to leave at that point and the car pulls away. It is too late, though. Everyone is looking at me and laughing. 'Everyone' being the VTs and their sidekicks who have miraculously reappeared as if drawn like magnets to my public humiliation. And peeking over their shoulders is Aubrey.

My stomach falls as though I am in a rollercoaster doing loop-the-loop. I reach back and grab at my skirt and yank it. My face burns while I pray no one saw my knickers.

My prayer falls on deaf ears. Or rather, it has the opposite effect: there is a pop and a slightly tearing sound as the button pings off the waistband of my skirt. I have pulled at the fabric too hard. My skirt comes away in my hands and falls to the ground before I can stop it.

I shriek and drop into a crouch to gather my skirt back up again. Never in my life have I wanted to fall through a portal into another world so much as I want to now.

'We can definitely see your pants now, Skye!' says Livvy.

I can't get up. I am curled in a ball, clutching my skirt

to me, willing the bell to ring, for a teacher to come – anything to get everyone to move away from me.

'Yeah – what are you doing?' says Izzy. 'Auditioning for one of your mum's Latin dance routines? You're not supposed to rip your *own* skirt off. You're supposed to have a partner to do that.'

'Ha! Maybe she was hoping that hot Finn Parker would do that for her,' says Livvy.

Tears are threatening to spill down my cheeks. I blink hard and bite my lip. I can't let them see I am upset. I'm going to have to style this out somehow. I will get up and calmly walk past them all, holding my head in the air (and my skirt up too, obviously). It's no good, though, I can't make my legs work. *Why* doesn't the bell ring?

Then I hear Izzy say, 'Fat chance. Finn couldn't get away from *her* fast enough. What d'you reckon, Aubrey?'

At the sound of my best friend's name, I automatically look up. There is quite an audience encircling me now. The VTs are in the front-row seats of course, their thumbs frantically texting while they giggle and smirk. I am surprised their brains are big enough for such multi-tasking.

Oh flip. I am never going to get past this crowd. I urge myself to think of a quick come-back, a funny line to distract people from what has just happened.

Nothing.

Turns out I have lost the ability to speak as well as run.

'Your face!' squeals Livvy, pointing at me.

As if following a cue, everyone erupts into a chorus of mean cackles and hoots.

I swallow hard. How do the VTs know about the ballroom dancing? How can they do this to me? What have I ever done to them? I can't bring myself to look at their pinched, sneering crocodile smiles. I finally manage to get up, my skirt firmly held up with one hand. I search out Aubrey, who is standing just behind Izzy. I plead with my eyes that she will come to my rescue. She doesn't say anything; just shrugs and looks away, her cheeks pink. With what? Surely *she's* not feeling embarrassed?

Or guilty?

Did *she* tell them about the dancing? No. I can't believe my best friend would do that when she knows how I feel about Mum going to the classes. What would she get out of telling them that, anyway?

I swipe at my tears with my free hand and am finally about to form some words when the bell goes. At last.

Izzy, Livvy and their groupies give me one last look up and down before bursting out laughing again and turning to go to class.

'Mind you,' I hear Izzy say, as they walk away. 'I wouldn't want to be seen dead with any of that family.

Did you see what Skye's mum was wearing? Talk about a walking car-boot sale! It's enough to make you turn GREEN. Hahahaha!'

Aubrey mouths 'Sorry' and waits while the toxic twins and their gaggle of gargoyles walk past her. Then she comes up and puts her arm around me.

'Come on,' she says. 'Let's go to the nurse and get you a safety pin for your skirt. You mustn't listen to them. They just think they're being funny.'

'Yeah. Hilarious.' Tears are rolling down my face now.

'You OK?' she asks softly.

I don't trust myself to speak. I don't want the tears to get the better of me. What would I say in any case? I think about challenging Aubrey over how the VTs knew about the ballroom dancing, but she is being so nice to me now and I just want to get out of here. Fast.

Maybe she didn't tell them.

But if she didn't, then who?

My eye falls on Finn who is making his way to the Year 9 block.

It was him, I know it.

I will kill him.

'Yeah, I'm fine,' I say to Aubrey. 'Thanks for sticking with me,' I add with a watery smile.

Aubrey leans into me and gives my arm a squeeze. 'No worries,' she says. 'What are friends for? Besides,' she adds, 'now that I've saved you from the VTs, you owe me one.' There is a glint in her eye that I don't like the look of.

'I do?'

'You do . . .'

'Okaaay,' I say. 'So, what do you want from me?' The answer is already forming in my mind, but I am not going to be the one to say the words. I raise my eyebrows at Aubrey and wait while she clasps her hands together, grins from ear to ear and makes a funny little squeaking voice.

Here we go . . .

'Pleeeeease can you introduce me to Finn? I can't speak to him on my own. I *can't*!'

She certainly should get a prize for not giving up.

I let out a long, slow breath. 'Maybe,' I say finally.

Anything to shut her up.

Except it doesn't.

'Oooooh! She begins clapping her hands and squealing and jumping up and down, just like Pongo when you hold a doggy treat just out of his reach.

'I LOVE you, Skye Green!' she cries, giving me a monster hug.

And, somehow, that makes everything seem OK.

For now.

Chapter Twelve

The minute I have made the sort-of promise to Aubrey I begin to regret it. I already have visions filling my brain of Aubrey and Finn becoming a couple. I am perfectly aware of the saying 'Three's a crowd', and I can just see myself being left out in the cold while they build their little love nest together. (EEUUW!)

I decide I have to make a plan to divert Aubrey from any further thoughts of Finn.

I promise myself that the next time she tries to bring him up in conversation, I shall think of a startlingly interesting thing to say to distract her. I am not going to be tongue-tied again.

So when, after registration, we are scrabbling in our bags for our French books, and Aubrey leans over to whisper to me, I think to myself, I will be ready for this.

'So, when is Finn next coming to babysit? Because I think it would be better if you introduced me to him at yours rather than at school. So, what I thought was, I could come round and say I had to do my homework with you – which wouldn't be an entire lie, as we sometimes do that, and who knows, we might be given some homework to do in pairs anyway? And then I could offer to make Finn a cup of tea or something and that way we could get talking and I could maybe tell him The Hogs are looking for a new drummer and then maybe—'

'A cup of tea?' I blurt out. 'A cup of *tea*? Is that what those magazines suggest is the best thing to offer a boy you really like? Are you sure you haven't been reading *Women's Institute Monthly*?'

The trouble with plans you make in your head is that they have a habit of not working out so well in reality.

If Aubrey's eyes could shoot actual daggers at me, that is what they would be doing right now. 'OK, well if you have any better ideas, you had better let me know. Perhaps I should tuck my skirt into my pants and see if that gets his attention,' she snaps.

I immediately feel bad, because I don't know what I would have done without Aubrey there to save me this morning.

'I'm sorry,' I say. 'The thing is, Finn isn't coming round tonight anyway. Mum only goes to one class a week and she's already been this week. So—'

'But can I not come round anyway and maybe – I

don't know – you could ask him round to hang out with us while Harris watches TV?'

This is awful. How am I going to get her to shut up about this? I am going to have to change the subject altogether.

'So, that text you sent me was a bit freaky,' I say. 'You know, "Had a great time" – at the dentist's? Seriously?'

Not very smooth of me I know, but hey, desperate times and all that . . .

Aubrey's face twists into an unreadable expression. I think she is about to have a go at me for trying to divert her away from talking about Finn when she says, 'Yeah, well. I was – er – trying to be funny. You know, like – no one likes going to the dentist, right? So I thought, I'll pretend it was fun. Ha ha.'

'Oh yeah. I can hardly breathe, I am laughing so much,' I say.

Aubrey smiles. 'I know. Must have been the painkillers I had to take after he gave me a filling – messed with my sense of humour or something.'

'Right.' I don't know what she is talking about, but I put it down to my best friend being quirky, which she sometimes is, and I settle down for a lesson of learning how to describe my house in French. As if I will ever have to do that in my entire life. What French person says, 'Hello. Please describe your house to me'? Unless they are trying to burgle it, in which case I would definitely not go and describe it, would I?

Sometimes I wonder what school is actually for. I would learn a whole lot more at home, reading the books I want to read.

By lunchtime I have managed to divert Aubrey away from talking about Finn a further three times. I have used the 'Did you see that bonkers programme on telly last night?' trick; the 'I HAVE to show you the cute kitten clips I found online the other day' trick; and the 'Come to the library with me, I need more books' trick.

Aubrey has mercifully fallen for all three of them. So at lunchtime we are in the dining hall, munching our pasta and talking about what a nightmare it is when your favourite book is made into a film. (Because, let's face it, it is *never* going to turn out how you imagined it in your head – I mean, Mr Beaver played by Ray Winstone speaking with a London accent in the film of *The Lion, the Witch and the Wardrobe*? WRONG, plain wrong, I am telling you.)

Things are almost starting to feel like normal between us when, horror of horrors . . . the VTs make a beeline for our table.

'No!' I say through gritted teeth. 'Don't look now but Dr Frankenstein's two latest monsters are headed our way.'

'Who?' says Aubrey, looking up. 'Oh, hi!' She waves. 'What are you *doing*?'

'Just being friendly,' says Aubrey.

'Right, well I'm off.' I stand up. I'm not staying to listen to what gems of sarcasm the VTs have been saving up all morning.

'Don't go,' says Aubrey. Although I'm not entirely sure she sounds as though she means it.

'It's crumble and custard for dessert,' I say. I may as well get some as an excuse for leaving the table.

'Ooh. Get me *some*,' says Aubrey, beaming.

'Yes,' says Livvy as she approaches. 'Get us some too, would you, Skye?' and flashes me a sugary smile. 'We promise we won't make any jokes about this morning,' she adds.

Right, so she's turning me into her slave as a bribe.

''Kay,' I grunt. 'Be back in a minute.'

I fix my eyes on the food counters so that I don't have to make eye contact with the VTs, and join the end of the queue. I am just wondering how I will be able to balance four helpings of crumble and custard on one tray when I hear someone say, 'Hey.'

I look up and see Finn. Can this day get any worse?

'Wow. You look in a good mood,' he says. 'Are you always so grumpy, or do you just save it for me?'

'Haven't you got anyone else to stalk?' I mutter.

He laughs. 'Not right now, no.'

I chew the sides of my mouth. What can I say to make him go away? If Aubrey sees me talking to him, she'll come over and then I'll have them both round at my house every evening and before I know it they will probably be smooching on the sofa. (HIDEOUS THOUGHT ALERT!)

I have reached the front of the queue and I'm loading my tray with four portions of dessert. Knowing my luck, Finn will say something clever such as, 'On a cake diet, are we?'

'So listen,' he is saying. 'I'm sorry about what happened this morning. You shouldn't take any notice of people like the twins. People who post videos of other people's accidents should be shot if you ask me—'

'Videos? *What?*' I whirl round in shock, wanting to find out *exactly* what video he is talking about.

Unfortunately I forget I am holding a tray full of crumble and custard.

'Watch it!' Finn shouts.

But it is too late. Four bowls of hot dessert have flipped up in the air. I watch in disbelief as they seem to slow down and then speed up as they fall towards me.

I am soaking. Dripping. Bathed from top to toe in hot, slimy, yellow gunge.

And everyone is laughing at me. For the second time today.

Chapter Thirteen

I am sitting in my room. I have barricaded the door so that no one can come in. I am thinking of never coming out ever again. Although that would make the need to eat, wash and have a pee pretty tricky. But I am not going to dwell on that now. I have far too much else to think about.

I thought the school day would never end. I ran out of the hall and headed to the loos after the Custard Incident. All I could think was: I need to hide! Everyone was pointing at me and laughing – some people were even on their feet clapping and whooping. Luckily I had so much custard in my eyes that I couldn't see that clearly, so I missed the expressions on their faces. I bet a load of them got the whole thing on their phones. I shall probably be having flashbacks for the rest of my life and need to go into therapy.

Mind you, then I could write a book about it. Mrs Ball the librarian says that 'everything is material' for a writer, which means that even bad things that happen can be turned into stories.

Still, thanks to the VTs, all my 'material' has been taken already and TURNED INTO VIDEO CLIPS! Finn said he had seen a video of the Pants Incident posted online already. Of course! I have just realized: they weren't *texting* while I was holding on to my clothes and trying to make a break for it. They had just filmed me and were posting the clip to YouTube!

Oh my life. I am so stupid. I am never going to be able to walk the streets in the hours of daylight ever again.

Once in the loos, I tried in vain to wash the custard off my clothes by splashing water from the basin at myself and rubbing my shirt with handfuls of paper towels. I put my head under the taps to rinse my hair and then stuck my head under the hand dryer. I heard some familiar cackling headed my way, though, so I had to give up and dive into a cubicle. There was no chance I was going to allow myself to be cornered by the VTs in there. They would probably grab me and flush my head in a loo or something. And film it too. That is how stylish and unoriginal they are with their bullying techniques.

I put the loo seat down and sat on it and drew my feet up and hugged my knees close: I wasn't taking any chances. I didn't want them to spot my feet. I kept my breathing as shallow as possible and listened.

What I heard did not make me feel any better about life. In fact, it made me feel significantly worse.

Livvy (or Izzy) was giggling and saying, 'That was soooo epic! I already had one hundred and nine likes for the Knickers In A Twist video and now we've got two hundred and three for the Custard Catastrophe! Skye-Blue-Pink-Face really is a goofball.'

'Yeah,' said Izzy (or Livvy), 'but remember she is the only one who knows Finn Parker. I think Aubrey's right, we should be being nice to her if we want to hang out with Finn. He's never

going to talk to us Year 8s unless we get Skye
to introduce us.'

'Right. Cos that has sooo worked for Aubrey,'
said Livvy (or – whatever – I can't tell them
apart when I can't see them). 'Aubrey said she
was going to get to meet Finn when we saw her
yesterday in town, remember? She said that the
next time Skye's mum does *ballroom dancing* –'
at this point she broke off to indulge in some
more insane giggling – 'BALLROOM DANCING!
Anyway . . . the next time she did that, Finn
was going to be round at Skye's, and Aubrey
was going to go round too.'

'Hmm,' said Izzy. 'We should go and find
Aubrey right now, don't you think?'

Then there was a dramatic gasp. 'Look!' said
Livvy, and clearly gestured at something. 'That
has given me the BEST IDEA!' she squealed.
'What do you think?'

My stomach had fallen through the floor. I
could hardly make sense of what I had overheard:
'. . . *yesterday in town . . . she said Skye's mum
does ballroom dancing.*' I held my breath as they
left the girls' loos, giggling and plotting.

I stayed in the cubicle until the bell rang and then waited until the last possible moment to slink back into class. I sat at the back while Mr Needham droned on and on about electricity.

I spent the whole lesson trying to work out what was going on. The VTs said they had seen Aubrey 'yesterday in town'. Did this mean she hadn't been to the dentist at all? Or did she just bump into the VTs? But what about that text saying 'Had a gr8 time this afternoon'? She behaved really awkwardly when I asked her about it. What if she had meant to send it to one of the VTs instead of me?

She must have seen them because they said Aubrey had told them about Mum's ballroom-dancing craze.

So this means that my best friend has been lying to me. I bet she didn't even go to the dentist at all: I bet she was in town, hanging out with the VTs all along. In fact, the more I think about it, the more I realize she has been going behind my back for a while. First she goes to the disco without me, then there's some story about the cinema, and now this.

☆ ☆ ☆ ☆ ☆ ☆ ☆ ☆ ☆ ☆ ☆ ☆ ☆ ☆

It is suddenly all very clear: Aubrey does not want my friendship any more.

Unless she gets something out of it: i.e. Finn.

What am I going to do? My life well and truly sucks.

☆ ☆ ☆ ☆ ☆ ☆ ☆ ☆ ☆ ☆ ☆ ☆ ☆ ☆

Chapter Fourteen

Feels like the only 'person' I can trust is my journal, so I am in my room, writing again.

The last couple of days have been like this: get up and bolt breakfast so that I can hassle Mum to take me and Finn into school early. Get there before the VTs so that I don't have to face them or any of their sidekicks seeing Mum in whatever unearthly creation she has decided to wear that morning. Hang out in the library until the last possible moment before class so that I can avoid speaking to Aubrey.

I should probably stand up to Aubrey and tell her I know that she has been lying to me. I should also tell her that I am never going to introduce her to Finn. But if I do either of those things then I will definitely lose her for good. But then if I DO introduce her to Finn I will lose her too. Maybe I should face the fact that I have lost her anyway. Do I even want to be friends with someone who can be so two-faced?

That's the thing, though. Of course I do. It's Aubrey.

I am so confused. I think the best thing for me to do is to bury my head in a book. So far this term I have already read three Lemony Snickets, two John Greens and a Cathy Cassidy. Bit of a mixture (and all quite sad books too) but I don't really care. I just need to go somewhere in my head that is not Real Life. Maybe I should reread the Cathy Cassidys. She is really good on friendships and heartbreak. I might pick up some tips on how to get myself out of this mess.

I don't know. I think maybe I prefer not to think about it any more just at the moment.

At least at school I have been able to hide at break and lunch. Mrs Ball has been great and given me loads of library duties to do, so it has been easy to come up with reasons as to why I need to be in the library.

I have been in survival-mode, keeping well

below the parapet, ducking to avoid any VT-shaped pieces of shrapnel that might come my way. I seem to have done OK so far. Thank goodness it is Friday so I only have to survive one more day before I can go into full-hermit-mode over the weekend.

Here goes: time to leave my writer's turret and brave the reality of the Big Bad World . . .

I head straight for the library. I don't even want to talk to Aubrey at registration at the moment. Maybe I could find a quiet corner and do some more writing. Just some notes on scrap paper: I haven't brought my journal to school. I am not that stupid. Imagine what the VTs would say if they found it? Imagine what they would do with it? It literally makes me shudder to think.

I am feeling on a roll with my writing at the moment, though. Or 'In the Zone' as I think writers say.

I might just check the display board first. I have been helping Mrs Ball over the past two days, decorating the board to promote the Alex Rider series. Maybe I could add a few finishing touches. I am pretty pleased with how it is shaping up, actually . . .

WHAT?

I am staring at the board, blinking and shaking my head in case I am imagining it, but no, this is no hallucination. There, right in front of my eyes, slap bang in the middle of all my hard work, is a poster. It is screaming at me in large, red and black letters:

Electric Warthogs introduce their new drummer: FINN PARKER!

Under the words, in glorious technicolour, blown up to magnify the cheesiness of his pleased–with–himself grin, is a photo of the boy who has come between me and my best friend.

It seems I have been so busy playing at being invisible that, clearly, I have not noticed what has been going on right under my nose . . .

I go cold. This is exactly the kind of disastrous scenario I was worried about: Finn becoming some kind of school hero, which is basically what getting into a band seems to do to people. (I think of the way Aubrey has started flapping her hands and hyperventilating any time anyone mentions Going Nowhere Fast – the band that has ironically been at number one for months.)

Oh no. Thinking of Aubrey like this has reminded me of something. I replay some of the things Aubrey has said: she was really excited when she found out that Finn plays the drums . . . She even mentioned that he might get into the school band . . . Did *she* put him up to this while I was hiding away in the library? Have they already hooked up? I should have done something, said something, anything to stop this happening!

I am stopped in mid-panicky-thought by the sound of footsteps skittering down the corridor behind me accompanied by chattering and high-pitched laughter.

I turn my head slowly to look through my fringe, but I already know who it is.

Voldemort and Voldemort. With my ex-best friend Aubrey, scurrying in their wake like a sugar-crazed weasel. The twins are arm in arm, almost skipping as they chatter. Aubrey is trotting behind, her head bobbing up every so often as she tries to keep up with them.

As they get closer I hear Izzy (or Livvy – I can't tell the difference at a distance) saying, '. . . so *cool* if the band said yes. D'you reckon we could be backing singers?'

'Yeah,' simpers Aubrey. 'It would be awesome to all be in the band together.'

'No!' I say, without thinking.

The twins stop in their tracks. As one, they face me, their arms still linked. They narrow their eyes and prepare to deliver one of their killer blows, like an alien creature with two identical heads.

Why did I speak?

I make a belated attempt to hide, ducking down behind a life-size cardboard cut-out of Alex Rider that Mrs Ball has put next to the display I was working on. I forget how flimsy it is and it wobbles as I catch the edge of it with my hand. I lunge forward to stop it falling, but I am too late. It topples towards the VTs and I end up on top of it, at their feet. My arms are wrapped around Alex Rider, my hair is all over my face and my skirt is rising dangerously up the back of my legs. At least Mum has sewn the button back on. I fling my hand back and tug it to stop it riding up any more.

'Oooh, look at that,' sneers Izzy, whipping her phone out. 'Skye is snogging Alex Rider. No need to throw yourself at him, Skye.'

Livvy cackles. 'Bit of a *two-dimensional* boyfriend, don't you think? But then, that's probably the only kind of boyfriend Skye-FALL will ever get her hands on.'

Aubrey laughs.

I push the cardboard figure off and get up, adjusting my clothes. I cannot bear to see Aubrey enjoying this. I square up to her.

'What are you doing, staring at me like that?' I snap.

'Nothing,' she says. 'Are you OK?' she adds, biting her bottom lip.

'As if you care!' I say.

Aubrey's face drains of colour and she turns away from me. She flicks her hair back, juts her chin in the air and says to the VTs, 'So: shall I see if Finn thinks the band could use us? I was talking to him yesterday. I'm sure I can get him to ask the rest of the band.'

I have to stop myself from gasping and shouting, 'TRAITOR!'

The twins visibly perk up at Aubrey's suggestion and immediately stop fiddling with their phones. It's like they have had a complete personality change, making room for Aubrey, moving to either side of her, cosying up, taking her arms in theirs.

I can't believe this. We have always hated the VTs. We have spent as long as I can remember (since Reception, pretty much) avoiding them and their mean tricks, fantasizing about how we could get our own back on them.

Why is she trying to get in with them now? What have I done to deserve this?

Aubrey raises one eyebrow at me and gives me a smile as if to say, 'Get me and my new best friends.'

I swallow hard. I have to say something. I can't be a total pushover. I scrabble around for an idea – anything that will make my friend take notice of me again.

'You – er – you were talking to Finn?' I say. My voice

sounds choked. 'I thought – I thought I said *I* would introduce you.'

Aubrey's smile turns acid. 'Yeah. Well you haven't, have you? Livvy and Izzy said they would come with me to tell him that The Hogs were auditioning for a new drummer. It was the perfect excuse to start a conversation.'

'The H-Hogs?' I stammer.

'Oh for goodness sake,' says Livvy. 'THE ELECTRIC WARTHOGS – The Hogs – that's what everyone calls them.'

'I know that,' I muttered.

'Yeah, like, *right*,' says Aubrey, rolling her eyes.

Izzy titters.

'The Hogs have been desperate for a drummer for ages, so they really need him,' Livvy goes on.

'He's going to have to bring his own kit in,' Aubrey says. 'He said he'd have to wait until his dad could bring it as it's too big for your mum's *tiny car*,' she adds.

Wow. She really is feeling nasty.

'Cool,' Livvy breathes. 'Tell us when and we'll come along. He is so dreamy, isn't he?' Her eyes go glassy. How does she do that? What a drama queen.

The three of them start giggling again and all start talking at once.

'Has he got a girlfriend, d'you reckon?'

'What kind of music is he into?'

'Do you think he'd come to our birthday party?'

It seems my wish to become invisible has been granted. Shame that didn't work when I was covered in custard or sprawled on the floor with my skirt in the air.

I take a deep, shuddering breath and focus on not letting the tears that are hovering behind my eyeballs spill out on to my cheeks. There is no way I am going to give these three witches the satisfaction of seeing me cry.

Luckily the thought 'these three witches' makes me think of the witches in *Macbeth*, dancing around their cauldron and throwing in eyes of newts and toes of frogs. The image is enough to stop me from blubbing outright, and I focus on that, mentally adding a few warts and gnarled bony fingers to the scene in my head, as I turn my back on my best friend and head into the library where I am soon hidden behind a bookshelf.

And there, my face safely shielded by a huge atlas, I give in to my feelings, and I cry silently, my shoulders heaving.

Chapter Fifteen

Saturday. At last. Usually I would be spending it hanging out at Aubrey's or she would come here. That is not going to happen, though. I doubt it will happen ever again.

Aubrey has not replied to a single text and hasn't spoken to me at all after the Alex Rider Incident: otherwise known as 'hashtag Skye-FALL', of course. Not that I have seen it. I am not going to torture myself by watching all those clips and photos the VTs have uploaded. I have checked my phone for texts at least a million times, though. I am even beginning to imagine the ping that lets me know she has texted. I think I am going insane.

Things got worse yesterday afternoon. Livvy clearly thought her joke was so genius she had to share it with everyone. That particular photo got over 300 likes, according to one of the VTs' groupies, who couldn't wait to let me know. I can't really blame Aubrey for not wanting to hang out with me: it would result in social suicide.

I can't bear to think about this any more. If I do I will end up blubbing, and then Mum will hear and she'll come into my room and want to know what the matter is. I am so not telling her what's going on, because she would only go and ring Aubrey's mum to try and get us to talk and fix things. That's what she used to do when we had the kind of tiny fights little kids have, like: 'She took the My Little Pony from my Happy Meal so we are never going to be friends ever again.'

I would kill for a fight like that. Those sort of fights were usually solved with a sleepover with Disney DVDs and ice cream. Somehow I don't think that's going to work this time. Which is a shame, as I still love Disney DVDs and ice cream.

I bet Aubrey does too. When her new best friends aren't looking.

So this weekend I reckon I am going to spend

as much time as I can in my room, reading (and writing, of course). Once I am deep into a book, I can make the world around me disappear. Although it is harder these days, what with the RACKET from Finn's drumming coming through the walls. He has been practising more and more since he joined The Hogs, and I guess it is only going to get worse as they prepare for their next gig.

Luckily I am reading a fantastic book called *I Capture the Castle*, which is so good I find it easier than ever to shut out my surroundings when I am 'in' it. It is by Dodie Smith who also wrote *The Hundred and One Dalmatians*, but personally I think *I Capture the Castle* is even better.

It is about a very intelligent girl called Cassandra who lives in a mad house with a family who doesn't understand her. She keeps a diary in which she writes about how frustrated she is with her life. I feel that we have a lot in common.

I think I am going to sit on the windowsill and write today. This is the kind of thing Cassandra does, except that she lives in a romantic, tumbledown castle in the middle of the countryside with a dad who is a writer and a stepmother who is a bohemian artist, whereas I live in a boring town house in a cul-de-sac with a mum who is a nutter and a brother who likes to dress up and sleep in the dog's bed.

(Maybe we don't have too much in common on the surface, Cassandra and I, but our view on life is pretty similar, let me tell you.)

Actually I think I might give up writing for today and read instead. It is very comfy up here. The windowsill is just about wide enough for me to sit on. I'll fetch a cushion to sit on, to stop my bum going numb, then I'll snuggle down. Peace at last.

The peace doesn't last for long. I am deep into the story (I have just got to the bit where the bohemian stepmum, Topaz – epic name! – dyes everyone's clothes green) when there is a racket outside my room and Harris comes crashing in.

'Skye, look! Look at this!' He is dressed from top to toe in what looks like silver foil. He is whirling round and round so fast I can't take him in properly, so I am not sure exactly what he is wearing. He appears to be holding on to something which looks as though it is also covered in silver foil. All his movements are accompanied by a loud rustling and crunching noise.

Gollum, who has been curled up on my bed, shoots in the air at the noise, hissing and spitting, before wisely scurrying under my bed to hide. I wish I could fit under there with her.

'Go away!' I have to raise my voice to be heard above the cacophony. 'Harris? HARRIS!'

Harris stops abruptly and is evidently very dizzy as he lands, with a heavy thud, on to the floor.

'Raaaooooowwf!'

That is when I notice that the silver thing that Harris has been holding on to was in fact Pongo.

'What are you *doing*, you insane child?' I ask, hands on hips.

Harris gets up, saying 'Ow' and rubbing his bottom, while Pongo does his best to extricate himself from sheets and sheets of silver foil.

'You do realize this is cruelty to animals?' I say, pointing at the poor pooch. 'I could report you to the RSPCA for this.'

Why that animal puts up with my brother, I do not know. I look at Pongo who is now eating some of the foil. Actually I think I *do* know why the dog puts up with

Harris: it is because he has about as much brain as my brother. Pongo looks at me as if he knows I am thinking about him. He wags his tail and sends shreds of foil up into the air.

Harris laughs. 'Pongo is making that confetti stuff that they have on the dancing programmes.' He scoops up a handful of silver and throws it over his head and begins spinning again, whooping with joy.

'HARRIS!' I yell.

My brother stops in mid-spin and falls over. 'Do you like my outfit?' he asks, sticking his head up from a mountain of silver foil. 'Pongo and I are practising our routine.'

'What in the name of normal are you talking about?' I say.

Harris frowns. 'The dancing competition, of course,' he replies. 'Haven't you been listening to Mum? She's entered a competition and so she needs to practise and I've said I'll help her – and Pongo too, of course. I've been training him.' He turns to the dog and commands: 'Pongo, up!'

At the sound of his name, our silly dog stands on his hind legs and holds his front paws up as though he is begging. Even I have to admit he looks cute, but I am not going to give my idiot brother the benefit of the doubt.

'It's ridiculous that Mum's entering a competition,'

I say. 'She's never going to be good enough for a competition, however many lessons she has. She'd better not be expecting us to go and watch her,' I mutter.

Fact: I would rather eat spiders.

'Of *course* we are going to watch her. And she is going to win because we are going to help her,' says Harris. 'Come on, Pongo!' He takes the dog by his front paws and drags him out on to the landing while singing some random song in a high-pitched tuneless voice. Pongo joins in, yapping and panting.

Turns out Britain Has Not Got Talent in this house.

I listen as the cacophony fades into the distance. Once I am sure they are not going to come crashing in again, I get comfy with my book and soon I am worrying with Cassandra about leaking roofs and batty stepmothers, and I have forgotten all about my own worse-than-batty family when . . .

BRRRRRIIIIIING!

The sound of the doorbell jolts me back to reality.

I hear Harris yell, 'I'll get it,' then the sounds of the door opening to the accompaniment of much silver-paper rustling.

The next thing I hear is far from welcome news.

'YAY! It's Finn! Hi, Finn, come in! SKYE, IT'S FINN! MU-UM . . .' And Pongo starts barking, joining my brother in his frenzied greeting.

Nonononono. This is the last thing I want – Finn coming round, no doubt to brag about being in the band. Harris will love him even more. In fact he will probably be so excited he will insist on showing him his bonkers silver-foil dance and then Finn will tell everyone at school that not only am I a walking disaster area but I also have a brother who is one sandwich short of a picnic. He might even film Harris and post it online to add to the ever-growing collection of Greatest Hits currently doing the rounds.

I can't face another moment of humiliation in my life.

Without thinking, I run into the bathroom and slam and bolt the door. I intend on staying in here and reading until Finn gets the message that I don't want him in my house.

I am about to get comfortable with my back to the radiator and my bum on a couple of towels when I realize I have left my book in my room. Sighing, I go to unbolt the door.

Except that I can't. Something has happened to the bolt. It is wedged shut.

I can't move it.

I rattle it and jostle it and rattle it again, but it won't budge. This is crazy. I must be doing something wrong. This has never happened before.

I tell myself to breathe, and have another go.

I try easing the bolt carefully back, forcing myself to slow down, to concentrate, not to worry.

It's no good. The bolt is stuck.

My chest is fizzing with sharp little bubbles of panic. I let my head fall forward as I take deep breaths and tell myself to think. And then I see that a screw has fallen to the floor. I pick it up and inspect it, looking at the bolt more closely, and I see that the screw must have been holding the bolt in place. Now that it has come loose, the bolt is wedged at a slight angle in the locked position. I try to ease the fixture back to its original position, but it just slips down again with the bolt securely stuck in 'locked' mode.

I bang on the door and shout, 'Can someone come and help me? I'm . . .' And then I stop.

I can't yell out that I am stuck in the bathroom because Finn will hear. I can just imagine what he will do with this knowledge once we are back at school. He would probably film this as well. Then the VTs could add it to their Classic Compendium of Comedy Clips. This would get even more 'likes' than the Skye-FALL video.

The Day Skye Green Got Stuck In The Loo. Sounds like the title for a really bad film. I can see it now. Boy, will they have fun thinking of things to Tippex on my locker after this.

WHY is this happening to me? *Why* did he have to come round?

Tears well up in me just like they did yesterday in the library. I won't cry. I ram the heels of my fists into my eye sockets. What if they do come and get me out and I am covered in snot and tears and my face is bright red? I will look even more of a baby than I already do – locking myself in the loo, crying for my mummy to come and get me out.

I slide down to the floor with my back against the door and sit, my knees drawn up to my chest. As I do so, I feel my phone sticking into me. I pull it out of my front pocket and see that Aubrey has messaged me. More than once. I have had my phone on silent while I have been reading, so I didn't notice the texts come through.

What if she is texting to say how much she hates me?

But why would she bother doing that?

Maybe she is texting to apologize?

Doh! I can't sit here, locked in the loo, just staring at my phone like this. I may as well read the texts. If the first one is mean, I can just go through and delete the lot without reading the rest.

I hold my breath and open the first one.

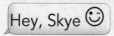

Hey, Skye 😊

OK so far, I guess. Although 'Sorry for being mean yesterday' might have been a better opener. Still, beggars can't be choosers, as they say. I read on.

> Am SOOOOOOO bored.
> Shopping with Mum & Cora 😺

I can't help smiling at this. I can imagine that Aubrey is tearing her hair out shopping with her sister and mum. I can't think of a worse way to spend a Saturday.

OTHER THAN BEING STUCK IN THE BATHROOM WHILE MY NEXT-DOOR NEIGHBOUR CASTS HIS WICKED SPELL ON MY ENTIRE FAMILY.

Another text pings through as I am staring at the screen.

> Soz about yesterday. I was being a dweeb. Forgive me? #BFF 😺

I feel a pang of shame that I doubted my friend. My heart goes melty-soft. I don't know if it's the word 'dweeb', which is one of our favourite words for describing how we feel when we have messed up. Or maybe it's the cute-face emoticon. Or maybe it's just that right this minute I could do with my best friend realizing that she has made a huge mistake.

Then I think: It's all my fault anyway. I pretty much ignored her and avoided her for two days solid at school. Also, I did actually kind of promise to introduce her to Finn . . . and then I didn't. What sort of a friend am I?

No wonder she blanked me.

I should have paid her more attention. I should have stuck to her like glue.

Another text pings up.

Where R U? Txt me! Need news. Am dying on Planet Shopping Mall. 🐱

I giggle at this and decide to text back; something random that does NOT involve anything about the VTs or Finn or us falling out or . . .

A pounding on the door makes me leap up in shock and drop my phone.

'What?' I say.

'Hurry up!' It's Harris. 'I'm desperate.'

'Go to the downstairs loo,' I tell him.

'Can't – Finn's in there,' he replies. Then he adds, 'He's so cool! He's taught me how to whistle through my fingers. Listen!' He lets forth a whistle which is so ear-piercing I am very pleased that there is a door between us.

'You can't be that desperate if you can whistle like that,' I say.

'But I am!' says Harris. 'In fact, oh no! I think I am even more desperater now.' I can hear him jumping up and down and picture him crossing his legs. Not a good mental image.

'OK, look – I think I'm locked in,' I say, trying to keep my voice sounding calm and grown-up. 'So go back down, use the loo after Finn, and then ask Mum – WITHOUT Finn hearing – to come and get me out.'

'Eh?' says Harris.

'JUST GO AND GET MUM!' I say. So much for calm and grown-up.

Before Harris can reply I hear footsteps. Thank goodness. Mum will get me out while Finn is still . . . otherwise engaged.

'What's up?' says another, deeper voice.

Oh great. Just great. It's not Mum. It's Finn.

'Why are you jumping like that, buddy?' he is saying to Harris.

'Cos I need to pee and Skye wouldn't let me in cos she says she's locked in!' Harris whines.

'Okaaay,' says Finn. 'So why don't you go downstairs? I'll help Skye.' I can hear the amusement in his voice.

Yeah, right. I don't believe for one moment that he wants to help me.

Once Harris has run off, Finn starts laughing so hard I am thinking it is a good job he has already been to the loo, otherwise he might wet himself.

Another top mental image. Well done, Skye, you are surpassing yourself today.

'I am so glad I am such a great source of hilarity,' I say with as much sarcasm as I can manage. 'While you are enjoying yourself, do you think you could please go and get Mum?'

'Er, not really,' says Finn through his laughter. 'She's in her room trying on outfits for her next class.'

Give me strength. She is a woman obsessed. 'Okaaay,' I say slowly. 'Call through the door to her then.'

'No, I can't do that,' says Finn. 'It's weird. She might be in her underwear.'

'I said CALL through the door,' I shout. 'You don't have to go in.'

At this point Harris can be heard running back up the stairs.

'I've got an idea,' he says. 'Let's get your dad, Finn.'

'NO!' I yell.

'Why is everyone outside the bathroom?'

Ah, thank goodness. It's Mum.

'Mum! It's me, Skye,' I say.

'We know that,' says Finn, sniggering.

'SHUT UP!' I say.

'Skye, dear, that's not very nice,' says Mum. 'Why don't you come out instead of shouting at us through the door?'

'I can't! That's the whole point,' I say. 'The bolt's got jammed.' My voice wobbles. I bite my lip.

Do. Not. Cry.

'One of the screws has fallen on the floor,' I say. 'I'm stuck – can you get me out?'

Mum laughs. 'You silly sausage!' she says. 'What were you doing, bolting yourself in there anyway?'

Mum's laughter pushes a button inside me. The unshed tears are immediately replaced by a shot of pure, hot anger; my ears are ringing with it. How can she laugh at me in front of Finn?

'What kind of a question is that?' I shout. 'I bolted the door because I didn't want anyone to come in, of course. Just GET ME OUT, can't you? And don't call me a "silly sausage",' I add, my voice dropping to a sulk.

Finn, Mum and Harris are all laughing now. Then Finn says, 'I think Harris is right – I should get Dad. He's got a good toolkit.'

'NO!' I say.

They are not listening to me, of course. I hear Mum saying thank you to Finn and then their voices recede as they walk away.

I slide down on to the floor again and my phone beeps once more.

Another text from Aubrey:

> BORED BORED BORED. Pleeeeeeease text me. I am soooooo sorry if I have upset you 😿😿😿

It is such a relief to see my best friend's name that I automatically text back without pausing to think.

> My life WAY WORSE than yours. Am stuck in loo. 🙀😲☹️👎

Aubrey replies straight away.

> WHAT? 🙀😬👎

Thank goodness for my BFF.

I am soon engrossed in texting back and forth and telling Aubrey the whole sorry story. She is being really sympathetic and making me laugh with more emoticons and silly selfies. It feels good to be joking around with her again.

I have almost forgotten that I am stuck in the bathroom.

Until I hear voices again. A lot of voices. Oh my

LIFE. They have brought Rob. I can hear his deep voice over everyone else's.

This is it. I am going to have to face everyone laughing at me. May as well prepare myself.

I get up and put my phone on the shelf above the basin. I catch my reflection in the mirror and see I am looking stressed, so I rearrange my facial features into a suitably blank mask. Then I hear Rob saying he'll soon have me out of there and there is some giggling and simpering, which must be Mum.

'Hurray for Rob!' shouts Harris.

Give me strength.

'Stand back,' Rob says in a fake action–hero–type voice. 'We're coming in.'

Chapter Sixteen

There is a rattle and a thud, followed by a loud grunt as Rob shoulders the door. It springs open with more speed than I am prepared for.

It all happens so fast, there is no time to think. No time to stop myself.

Rob hurtles towards me.

I cry out and topple backwards. I feel myself falling but I can't stop the momentum. I am heading back towards the loo. I land on the seat with such force I fall back into it. Just my luck: the lid is up. I shriek as I feel my bottom sinks down. My arms flail up and my elbow catches on something painfully.

'Ow!'

Before I know it, there is a flushing noise.

I have landed in the loo and flushed it at the same time. Genius. You couldn't do it on purpose if you tried.

A crowd of laughing, grinning people bear down on

me: Harris is holding his sides he is laughing so much; Finn is guffawing too, and stabbing at his phone; Rob is trying to look concerned, but his mouth is twitching and . . .

Aubrey's here! Thank goodness. My best friend is here to save the day. She will make this all OK. She will give me a hug and we will get away from this nightmare.

Then I see she is frowning in concentration at *her* phone. She is not even looking at me.

I wriggle and try to get up while struggling to calm myself. Everyone is still laughing at me. I can't speak. Thought after thought rushes into my head: Why isn't Aubrey rushing to help me? Who is she texting now? It can't be me. Why is she here? How did she even get here so fast if she was shopping?

And then a chilling thought rushes in to override all the others: Maybe she wasn't shopping at all, in which case – has she been lying to me again?

Aubrey stuffs her phone in her pocket and makes a move towards me. As she does, I watch her rearrange her features into an exaggerated expression of pity.

'Aww, poor you,' she coos. 'It must have been soooo traumatic, getting locked in!' She offers me a hand. 'Let me help you.'

She pulls me rather too hard and I topple forward, water dripping off me. My jeans are soaked.

'Please,' I whisper. 'Get me out of here!'

Aubrey's eyes narrow. 'Not just yet,' she says through her smile (which has soured considerably now that no one else can see her face).

She raises her voice for the benefit of everyone else: 'Let me get you a towel,' she says.

'I – I'm fine,' I gasp, pushing at her to let me go.

'How did you know to come and help, Aubrey?' Mum asks.

'Oh, Skye texted me,' Aubrey says, before I have a chance to speak.

Finn does his irritating-snigger thing that seems to be his default setting. 'Texting from the toilet?' he says. 'Smooth.'

Aubrey rolls her eyes and gives Finn a sugary smile. 'I know,' she says.

Harris bellows with laughter. 'She takes her phone EVERYWHERE!' he says. 'I bet she even texts while she is actually wiping her bum!'

Mum smirks and rearranges her features unconvincingly to say, 'Harris, that's not nice.'

I take in her pink-and-purple satin ballgown and matching tiara and a little part of me dies inside. This whole scene is like something out of a weird circus act, and Finn and Aubrey have ringside seats.

Any more mortifying moments you would like to

throw at me, Universe? I think, as I watch them smirk and exchange knowing looks.

'Great. The freak show is over, you can all go home,' I mutter.

Mum clears her throat. 'Skye, dear,' she says, 'you could at least say thank you to Rob – and Aubrey.'

'Thank you, Rob,' I say. I cannot bring myself to look at him. At anyone.

'No worries,' he says. 'I – er – I'm really sorry you fell . . . I didn't think the door would be that flimsy.'

'You don't know your own strength!' Mum says, nudging Rob's arm.

'Yeah, Rob is really, really STRONG!' Harris says. He bounces up and down in delight. 'I reckon he could even lift you up, Mum. Like in those dances—'

Mum cuts him off with a fake laugh and says brightly, 'Go and get changed, Skye. I'll make everyone a nice cup of tea, shall I?'

Oh yes, great idea, I think, as I slip off to my room. Cos that's what all normal people do when their daughter has just flushed herself down the loo in public: hold a tea party. Why don't we crack open the bubbly while we're at it and have a full-on celebration?

I want to stay in my room once I'm changed, but I know Mum will only come and find me and tell me off for being antisocial. Or worse, Aubrey will come and find me and have a go at me. She looked so angry when she 'helped' me to get up. I shall just have to keep my head down so that I don't have to look at anyone.

I sneak quietly into the kitchen while everyone is chatting. Mum is fussing with the kettle, mugs and tea bags and laughing and enjoying herself like a hostess at a ball. (She probably thinks she *is* at a ball, dressed like that.)

Why can't everyone just leave?

Harris is so excited by the turn events have taken that he is now running round the table, still covered in silver foil, with Pongo, who has lost most of his foil by now.

Mum catches him as he goes past and says in a low voice, 'That's enough, sausage. And although your outfit is very – er – imaginative, can you take it off? It's rather loud and rustly.'

Rob laughs. 'What you are, Harris? A spaceman?'

That's right, let's all talk about Harris and then I can go back upstairs unnoticed and we can all forget about my latest performance on The Clumsy Klutz Show.

'No, I'm a dancer,' says Harris, beaming and giving a pirouette for good measure.

'Ah,' says Rob. 'Nice one.'

Finn ruffles Harris's hair. 'Harris is dancing with his mum, aren't you, mate?'

'Yeah!' says Harris. 'Mum's entering a competition

and I've said I will help.' He peels off a strip of silver foil and says, 'I need to think about the music she will use. Can you help me choose, Finn?'

'I'm sure Finn would be great at that,' says Aubrey. She does the whole dipping-head-fluttering-eyelashes routine. 'He's an awesome musician.'

Finn frowns. 'Nah. Not really.'

'Don't be so modest, Finn,' says Rob. 'Finn's learning the drums,' he says to Mum. 'Hopefully you won't be disturbed for long,' he adds hastily. 'I'm soundproofing the garage, but the drums are in the back room for now.'

'Amazing!' says Mum. She looks as thrilled as if Rob has announced that he has found a cure for cancer.

Rob is blushing now. 'Not really. I'm a builder by trade, you see. Well, more of a site manager these days. That is why we moved here – new job, you see.'

Great. So we are all going to drink tea and make small talk while I die of embarrassment and my brother prances around dressed in tinfoil.

I try to catch Aubrey's eye but she is too busy staring at Finn while he wrestles with Harris and Pongo. Surely she can see this is all a nightmare? Has she changed that much that she would rather watch a boy she doesn't know roll around with my brother than talk to me, her best friend?

I sidle up to her. She pretends she hasn't noticed and

sips her tea, keeping her eyes averted from mine.

'So,' I say quietly. 'I, er, I thought you were out shopping with Cora and your mum today?' Great opening line, Skye.

'Yes,' says Aubrey. She puts a lot of meaning into that one small word. 'I bet you did,' she says, through gritted teeth. 'Which is why you have *him* round –' she nods her head at Finn – 'without telling me!'

'What?' A fluttering starts up in my chest. 'You don't think – surely you don't think I *asked* him round?'

She turns and looks at me, one eyebrow arched. 'All I know is, you are always making promises you don't keep,' she says.

'So,' says Mum, clapping her hands together. 'Seeing as we're getting along so well, how about I make us all some lunch?'

Aubrey sends me a barrage of texts after she leaves while I remain hunkered down in my room. Most of them are along the lines of:

Can't BELIEVE you had Finn round for AN HOUR without telling me. 😺

I asked you to get me round to see him!!!! 😣
Y R U keeping him all to urself? 😼 👎 😣

And so on and so on.

I start by trying to tell her that things are not as they seem. This doesn't make any difference so I give up trying to explain. It is hopeless by text, in any case. Aubrey only sends back more and more angry emoticons in reply, including the red-faced devil cat ones and black clouds and bolts of thunder and lightning.

In the end she gives up on words altogether, so I ask her back round on Sunday, saying that we need to talk. She doesn't text back for ages and in the end I get one word: 'Busy'. And that is the last I hear from her until Monday at school.

Chapter Seventeen

I woke up this morning feeling sick to the pit of my stomach. It was the first day that the bus was running again because the roadworks in town have finished. I am on the bus now, keeping my head down and writing in my journal, not daring to look up. I managed to sprint to the bus stop and get on without seeing Finn, but what will I do if he has got on behind me and decides to tell everyone about the Loo Incident? What if Aubrey does? She really hates me now, I know she does. Those texts made it pretty clear.

How am I going to survive life at school without Aubrey? I don't know what to do without her. It is all very well when I am choosing to be alone, sitting in the library at lunch and break, but now that she doesn't want to speak to me at all, I feel like I will be on my own forever.

I have switched my phone off. There is no point in having it on: Aubrey was the only one who ever texted me and I don't want to be checking it all the time just to see that I (a) have more nasty messages from her, or (b) have no messages at all.

I don't know which is worse. We're at school already, so I'm going to have to stop writing.

I walk into the locker area, still hiding behind my fringe, and open my locker door fast so that I can hide behind that as well.

Someone comes up behind me and taps me on the shoulder as I am getting out the books I need for my first class. I turn round and come face to face with Aubrey, smiling at me. For a microsecond I think everything's going to be OK and I open my mouth to say something. Then the VTs appear on either side of her, like two pieces of rank burnt toast, popping out of a toaster.

'Hi, Skye,' says Livvy, flicking her long ponytail over her shoulder. Then she makes a big show of pulling a face and flapping her hand under her nose. 'Eeuw!' she cries. 'Anyone else smell that?'

'Urgh, yes!' says Izzy. 'It's like – there's a whiff of public loos or something.'

I turn back to hide in my locker.

'So, Skye. Been swimming in any more toilets recently?' Izzy says.

'Yeah. Called any knights in shining armour to rescue you?' I hear Aubrey add. Her tone of voice is almost identical to the twins'.

The VTs laugh, no doubt approving of Aubrey's oh-so-witty comment.

I feel my face flare and will my brain to come up with something clever and witty in reply, but all I can think is: Aubrey's not wearing her friendship bracelet.

I turn to look back at her and check both her wrists just to make sure. No, she has definitely taken it off.

'Your *face*!' crows Livvy. 'I don't know about Skye *Green* – you look more like Skye *Red* today.'

'Ha ha!' sneers Izzy. 'You know what they say about "red sky in the morning"? "That's a warning." Better stay out of her way before she explodes!'

I plead with Aubrey with my eyes to leave this evil pair and come back to me. There was a time not so long ago when a glance like this would have had Aubrey rushing to my side: she would have known exactly what I was thinking without me having to say a word. Like I say, we have always been able to read each other like a book.

Sadly, it turns out that today Aubrey is reading me completely wrong: instead of the Best Friends Make Up and Everyone Lives Happily Ever After story that I have in mind, she sticks her chin in the air, links arms with the VTs and says:

'I don't know what's happened to you these days, Skye. I think you need to get a life and grow up.'

This is what happens when you take off a friendship bracelet you have been wearing for nearly three years. You lose the power to read your best friend's mind.

I try one last attempt to get her to understand what happened at the weekend. 'Aubrey, it was not my fault about Finn. He came round to see Harris—'

'Oh, of course. Fit Finn Parker came round to play with your little squirt of a brother.' Aubrey snorts. 'I bet he did.'

I gasp. She has never said anything so mean about Harris before.

'You know what you've done, don't you?' says Livvy.

I say nothing. I have a feeling they are going to tell me the answer to this question, and I am not disappointed.

'You broke The Friendship Code, Skye Green,' says Izzy.

'Yeah,' says Aubrey, holding up her wrist to show me

what I have already noticed. 'You broke the code, and I have broken the bracelet.'

And our friendship, I think.

I can't make myself say it aloud, though. I beg my brain to think of *something* to say. Nothing happens. I feel numb. I turn my back on their laughter, praying that the bell will go and that I can leave it until the last minute to slink into class. I don't know where I am going to sit. I know one thing for certain, though: it won't be next to Aubrey, where I have sat ever since my first day at school.

The days of Aubrey and Skye are well and truly over.

Things got worse as the day went on. I should have seen it coming: turns out 'someone' managed to film the Bathroom Incident. It will have been Finn, of course. That must have been what he was doing with his phone while he was laughing at me. He probably even sent it to Aubrey straight away which is why she was checking her phone too. Or maybe it was the other way around and she sent it to him? Anyway, who cares which one of them did it? The VTs have already made sure it was posted in time for everyone to see it by lunchtime.

Everywhere I went people jumped out at me or crept up behind me and made flushing noises or shouted 'Boo!' and then said, 'Oh, *sorry* – didn't mean to make you wet yourself!' One clever person even went so far as to fill my locker with loo rolls so that when I opened the door at the end of the day, the whole lot fell on top of me. I wouldn't be surprised if that was caught on camera as well.

The only way I am going to survive at school from now on is by using the library as my safe haven. Mrs Ball keeps an eagle eye on anyone who goes in there. She has a zero tolerance policy on bullying. She has a superb tactic for keeping people in line: she eyeballs anyone misbehaving and talks them into signing up for The Summer Reading Challenge. Not a punishment for someone like me, of course, but the people who used to come into the library looking for trouble now know it is not going to work out in their favour, so they are staying away.

As I walked to the bus stop at the end of the day I heard Aubrey loudly talking to the VTs about going into town after school 'because The Hogs are going to McDonalds after their practice'.

Good luck to her. The VTs will only drop her the minute someone more exciting comes along.

I tell myself that, but I am not sure I believe it, and anyway, even if they do, will she ever want to come back from the Dark Side to be my BFF again?

Chapter Eighteen

As the days have gone by, life at home has become almost as bad as life at school.

The cherry of catastrophe has landed on top of the icing of disaster on my cake of doom.

Here is why: Mum bounced in after work one evening to announce that she was 'going to take some extra dance classes' because she thought she really had a chance in the competition but that she 'needed more practice'.

When I groaned, Mum asked, 'Why is that such a problem, Skye?' in a very annoyed tone.

Harris said he thought it was 'COOL' and had a go at me for being a 'grumpy old meanie'.

He would be a grumpy old meanie too if he had no friends and he was old enough to realize his mum is the most mortifying parent on the planet.

But then, Harris seems immune to embarrassment. In fact, he goes out of his way to out-perform Mum in that area of life.

For example, he has taken to carrying his old security blanket (fondly known as Bop-Bop for reasons lost in the mists of time) and waving it around like a cape while stamping in a circle around Pongo and shouting 'Olé'. He says he is determined to help Mum 'improve' her idiotic Latin-style dance. I have tried kindly pointing out to him that he will get teased mercilessly if he ever lets on about any of this to his mates at school. He just sticks his tongue out and tells me to mind my own business.

I have also said (a bit less kindly) that his act would be known as The Pongo instead of The Tango. It doesn't have any effect. He has been practising every night after school, with Finn encouraging him every time he comes round to babysit.

It is yet another dance-class night and Finn is due to come round any second. Mum has changed her outfit at least three times in the past ten minutes and is now asking my little brother's advice on what to wear. As if it matters. She goes to this class twice a week and presumably sees the same people who also dress like insane parrots. I doubt they notice from one session to the next what she is wearing.

'What do you think, little bean?' Mum is asking Harris. 'Gold and black, or red and black?'

'I think *both* are gorgeous,' says Harris, his eyes wide. He runs his fingers over the black feather boa Mum has flung around her neck. 'Can I have this after you've finished with it? Pongo would love it.'

Mum gives him an indulgent smile and tickles his face with the feather boa. 'No you can't!' she says. 'Pongo would most probably try to eat it – imagine the mess!'

'Awwwwwwooo,' Harris groans, his whole body collapsing with disappointment.

'What about you, Skye?' Mums asks me, holding her skirt out. 'Do you think the black-and-gold is too much? Because I could change the gold for red?'

She looks so anxious. I know I should say something nice, just as Harris has, but I can't think of *anything* nice to say to someone who looks like an ostrich who's been dragged through a rubbish tip backwards.

'Oh noooo,' I say. 'Gold is not too much. I am sure all the other dancers will look as though someone has wrapped them up and left them under the Christmas tree.'

'Skye,' Mum says, letting her hands fall to her sides. 'I don't know why you are so moody these days. You're always on Harris's case about his dancing as well. Are you jealous? Is that it? Maybe *you* should join a class—?'

'MUM!' I say. 'I do *not* want to learn how to dance. Two loonies in the family is quite enough – three if you count the dog. I can't bear the thought of us all dancing in a line in the town hall as if we are some kind of lame family entry for *Britain's Got Talent*.'

Mum laughs. 'Skye, you are so dramatic!'

I snort. 'Yeah, and you are not dramatic *at all*,' I mutter, nodding at her outfit. 'Why do I have to put up with Finn coming round to our house *twice* a week?' I add.

TWICE A WEEK.

Tuesdays AND Thursdays.

Kill. Me. Now.

'I mean,' I go on, 'why don't we all just move in together?'

'What makes you say that?' Mum snaps.

'Why not?' I say, flinging my hands in the air. 'We might as well. Finn practically lives here already anyway, and you are always chattering away to Rob as if he's your new best friend.'

'There's no need to be ridiculous,' Mum says. Her face is pink. Of course she's cross I am being moody, but I can't help it.

Then it strikes me: both Harris and Mum really have got new best friends. I am the only one who has *lost* a best friend. And the rest of my family doesn't seem to have noticed.

Mum gives a funny strangled cough and then says, 'I do think you are being silly, Skye. It is only a few hours a week. Is it really so much to ask?' Then she turns her back on me and goes into the kitchen to make a lot of noise with the washing-up.

I guess that means the matter is closed.

Why am I surprised?

No one is interested in anything I have to say any more.

Finn arrives just as Mum has changed back into the outfit she first had on and I immediately disappear to my room to let him get on with babysitting Harris. For 'babysitting' read: 'eating all the snacks, getting Pongo and Harris over-excited, and using up all the batteries in the house for monster Mario sessions'.

Finn is always raiding the other remotes and any

other device he can lay his hands on for batteries for the Wii, but guess what? I am the one who gets the blame when Mum goes to use her battery-operated electric toothbrush and it doesn't work.

It is no surprise therefore when I come down from solitary confinement under the duvet in my room to find Finn rummaging through the kitchen drawers. (I was reading *Carrie's War* – a story about kids who get evacuated to the countryside during the Second World War. I wish I could be evacuated to escape Aubrey, Mum, Harris, Finn, the VTs . . . and pretty much anyone else who knows me.)

'Hey, make yourself at home, why don't you?' I say. 'I guess you've eaten all our snacks already?'

Finn jumps at the sound of my voice, but quickly recovers with one of his trademark sniggers. 'Great look,' he says, nodding to my leopard-print onesie. 'Don't go jumping into the loo wearing that or the firemen might call the RSPCA when they have to come and get you out.'

'Ha very ha,' I say, deadpan. 'I did not "jump into" the loo last time and I have no intention of "jumping into" the loo at any point in the future. Anyway, what do the firemen have to do with it? I thought your superhero dad was only a call away to solve each and every problem for a damsel in distress.'

Finn pulls a face. 'Yeah, well, he's out tonight, isn't he?'

'Oh right. So I'm babysitting *you* then, am I?' I joke.

Finn's almond eyes glitter. 'No,' he says with feeling.

This is interesting. I had expected more of a comeback from him. Why is he looking uncomfortable? I scrutinize his face, waiting for more information, but none comes.

'So where's your dad gone?' I ask.

'Dunno. Just said he was meeting some friends,' Finn replies.

I am surprised by a feeling of pity that Finn's tone of voice arouses in me. He kind of sounds envious of his dad. As though he wishes he were out with friends too, instead of round at ours. Not that I would blame him for feeling like this. I wish *I* were out with friends. Flip, I wish I *had* friends to go out with. Finn at least has that – The Hogs, and probably even Aubrey and the VTs now as well. Everyone loves Finn Parker. So why does he look so sad all of a sudden?

It occurs to me that I have not bothered to ask him anything about his home life, about the move to our street, about his old school. I haven't asked him if he likes his new house, if he's glad he's moved – nothing.

Then again, he hasn't exactly opened up to me either. I haven't been round to his place, even though it's bang next door. Would I want to go if he asked? I wonder if Mum and Harris have been round while I've been hiding in my room. Would they go without me? I have been pretty moody lately. I guess I couldn't blame them if they had.

I watch Finn as he goes back to rootling through the mess of pens and old reels of Sellotape and broken pencils and rubber bands and paper-clips. He is frowning. Is he sad about something or is he just fed up with me and wants me to go away?

I have thought this before: it is a bit odd, a fourteen-year-old boy enjoying spending so much time with Harris. If he really does have so many friends, why does he still come round here? I guess he could use the money, but it is weird that he doesn't have anything else to do – that he's always available. Most of the boys in my class have endless footy practice. Maybe Finn isn't sporty. He doesn't seem that busy with The Hogs either, though, in spite of all the drumming practice I have been subjected to. I hear him most afternoons as soon as I get in from school. It is excruciating.

I feel suddenly ashamed that I have put all my efforts into disliking Finn and casting him as the enemy in my life, when really it's the VTs and Aubrey who are making life so horrible for me.

Maybe Finn really hates coming round here as much

as I hate having him here. Maybe Rob makes him. Maybe they need the cash?

I ought to make a bit of an effort.

'Erm, so how are you settling in?' I blurt out.

That was lame.

Finn doesn't sound off at me though – he merely shrugs. He is staring at his beaten-up high-tops, the dirty laces undone and trailing. He starts tracing a pattern on the tiled floor with his toe. He doesn't answer me, so I find myself babbling.

'I guess it must be cool having a builder for a dad – is he fixing up the house, decorating and stuff? He said he was going to soundproof the garage. That will be cool – for the band, I mean. Are you going to practise round at yours?'

What did I say that for? (a) That would mean I would hear even more of a racket than I already do unless Rob really is going to soundproof the garage; and (b) he probably thinks I want to crash in on him and The Hogs and become a groupie or something.

I need to put a brake on my mouth.

Finn is staring at me now. His expression is tricky to read. It's as if he is choosing his words carefully before speaking. It makes me feel uneasy: I don't know if he is about to tell me to shut up or even laugh at me.

He opens his mouth to say something but is interrupted

by Harris, who comes bowling into the room, dressed in the most eye-wateringly bad combination of clothes. He is lurching strangely from side to side as though there is something wrong with his legs. I can't actually see them under all the fabric.

'Ta-daaaah!' he says, making an awkward attempt at giving us a twirl. 'Don't I look fabulous?'

Harris is wearing Mum's clothes. A *lot* of Mum's clothes. He has a pink hairband in his hair to which he has fixed a red feather. On his top half is one of Mum's spangly tops and to cover the cleavage area (eeuw and double-eeuw!) which is clearly too large for Harris, he has carefully wrapped himself in one of Mum's long floaty scarves. On his bottom half he appears to be wearing at least two different sticky-outy ballgown-type skirts which he has hitched up to the right length by tying them round his waist with another floaty scarf.

It is this piece of fabric which Pongo is now doing his best to demolish, pulling it while he shakes his head furiously and growling as though he is the scariest dog in the world. (He really is not.)

To finish off this alarming outfit, Harris has borrowed a pair of Mum's second-hand DMs – the bubblegum pink ones. This would explain his inability to walk properly as they must be at least three sizes too big.

Finn is shaking with laughter. 'You kill me!'

Part of me is relieved to see Finn laughing at Harris rather than me.

The other part of me is appalled. All I can think is, Thank goodness Harris doesn't go to my school. A brother who dresses up in his mum's clothes and waltzes around with his dog would put the final seal on my reputation as a weirdo.

Harris is so happy he looks as though he might explode. 'Pongo and I are trying on outfits for Mum's competition,' he says breathlessly as he bounces up and down. 'It's really soon! Will you come with us, Finn?'

The clouds lift from Finn's face. I think he is about to say, 'Not on your life!' and carry on laughing, but instead he smiles and says, 'Yeah, sure!' He actually looks chuffed that Harris has asked him.

Why hasn't my brother asked me? I think.

'Harris,' I say. I have to raise my voice above the sound of his thumping feet and Pongo's growling and barking. 'You should put Mum's clothes away. She won't like it if you ruin them. She's not going to let you come to the competition with her, anyway. It will be way past your bedtime. And she certainly won't let Pongo come.'

'What do you care?' Harris says. He sticks his tongue out. 'You're not interested in dancing *or* Mum's competition, and you don't even *like* Mum's clothes.'

This is of course true, but I am trying hard to think

161

of some way of getting my brother to behave normally.

'Okaaay,' I say slowly. 'But I don't think it's a good idea—'

'Leave him alone!' says Finn. He has stopped smiling and his face has hardened. 'He's just having a bit of fun. You know what "fun" is, right?' he asks.

'Actually I do,' I say, squaring up to him. 'Or at least, I think I can remember what "fun" was like – it seems to have disappeared since you came to live next door.'

All my feelings of pity for him have vanished. How dare he talk to me like that in front of my brother? In my house? I actually feel as though I could slap Finn in the face right now.

He senses how angry I am and takes a small step back. Then he sniggers. 'I don't believe you've ever had any fun in your life, Skye,' he says. 'Especially not with that irritating little sidekick of yours hanging around.'

Harris has stopped prancing around and is staring at us. His freckled cheeks have paled. I am dimly aware that we are frightening him, fighting like this, when there are no grown-ups around for him to run to for support. But I don't care.

'What you do mean, my "sidekick"?' I say. 'I haven't got a "sidekick". I haven't even got a best mate any more, thanks to you and the Volde— Izzy and Livvy Vorderman.'

162

Finn's mean expression fades and his forehead creases. 'What?' he says.

'You and the twins – between you, you have stolen Aubrey away from me. You and your pathetic band, The Electric Warthogs. Flipping stupid name for a band as well!'

Finn looks startled. 'Hey, it's not *my* band—'

I am about to shout at him for being a miserable, lying, sneaky creep when there is the sound of a key in the front door, followed by the door opening and some laughter and chatter.

'Mum!' Harris cries, tripping over the jumble sale of clothes he has on and falling on Pongo in the rush to greet her.

It certainly is Mum's voice I can hear, but I can also hear someone else. It sounds like Rob.

Finn and I exchange puzzled glances, then remember we were fighting a couple of seconds ago and look away. Finn coughs awkwardly.

'Hi, guys!' Mum trills, coming into the kitchen. 'Hope you've had fun.'

Her eyes are shining and her cheeks are glowing. She looks like someone who has just got off the most fantastic, exhilarating rollercoaster ever.

Rob comes in behind her. He is looking smarter than usual. He's wearing a jacket and some dark jeans. He is beaming and chuckling. He looks as pumped up as Mum. Maybe they have just shared a joke. Must have been a pretty funny joke . . .

'All right?' he says to Finn. 'Good evening?'

Finn mumbles something I can't hear and slouches out of the room.

Rob's smile fades and he looks suddenly awkward. 'Teenagers!' he says to Mum. 'What can you do?'

Mum nods. 'Tell me about it. Skye's not even strictly a teen yet, although from her behaviour I think she is already in training.'

'Thanks a lot,' I say. 'So, how come *he's* here?' I ask, nodding to Rob. I know I am being rude, but Mum has annoyed me.

Mum frowns and says, 'Skye . . .' but she is prevented from saying any more by Rob, who has put a hand on her arm.

''S'OK,' he says quietly, shaking his head.

Mum reddens. Is she going to tell *him* to shut up as well?

Instead, though, she says, 'Rob was just – er – coming round to get Finn, weren't you?' she says. Then she turns brusquely, so that Rob's hand drops from her arm, picks up a pile of post on the work surface and begins riffling through it noisily.

Rob becomes brisk. 'Yup, that's right,' he says. 'Finn!'

he calls down the hall. 'Time to go, mate. School night and all that,' he adds for our benefit.

Finn appears sulkily in the living-room doorway.

'Awwwwwoo!' says Harris. 'Can't I come round for a bit to yours?' he asks, sidling up to Finn. 'You said you would let me play the drums last time I came round . . .'

'Nah, Dad's right,' Finn says. 'I should head home and you – ' he says to Harris, giving him a light punch on the arm – 'you need to go to bed.'

I am watching all this thinking, Last time I came round? So they *have* been next door without me. Even my own family is blanking me now . . .

'Yes,' says Mum, agreeing with Rob. 'Bedtime for both of you. You too, Skye,' she says. 'Although it looks as if I am going to have to disentangle my son from his rather unusual choice of clothing first.' She laughs in a light, fake way and starts bustling about, clearing away the remains of the snacks Finn and Harris have littered all over the table.

'OK, Finn,' says Rob. 'Let's go, buddy.'

As they leave, I watch Mum say goodbye and thank you, and hand Finn a tenner. I notice that shiny-eyed look on her face again. And then I realize she looks different from the old mum; the mum before the ballroom-dancing days. She looks happy; happier than I have seen her in a long, long time. I guess if the dancing makes her feel that good, I shouldn't be so mean about it. Harris really enjoys having Finn around too.

I find myself thinking that I am the only one around here who is miserable. Maybe it is no surprise that Aubrey doesn't want to be my friend any more. 'No one likes a misery guts,' as Mrs Robertson used to say.

Chapter Nineteen

It is Saturday. Another day on my own in my room. Just me and my windowsill. Mum and Harris are out in the front, gardening, and I am reading, as usual. I have just started an amazing fantasy called *The Owl Service* by Alan Garner. It is about a girl called Alison whose dad dies and her mum remarries a man with a son called Roger so Alison ends up with a stepdad and a stepbrother. It is not a happy arrangement. They go on holiday to try and 'bond' as a new family. I hope this never happens to us. I think about Mum saying she wanted to 'meet people' at her classes. At least she seems to have stopped talking about that. For now.

I am distracted by the sound of a van pulling up outside. I look up. It's not Rob's van. It's a camper van, decorated with multicoloured swirly patterns and flowers. This sparks my interest: no one around here has anything as cool as this. I sit up and press my face against the window.

I draw back almost immediately when I see Rob get out of the passenger side – and Finn follows, climbing out of the back. In spite of not wanting to have anything to do with next door, I can't help being intrigued. I pull my curtain forward and use it as a screen to peep out from. Who has driven them home? As if reading my thoughts, a super-pretty, tiny young woman comes round to the pavement side. She is smiling warmly and talking to both Rob and Finn, gesturing at the house. She has the longest, darkest, shiniest, straightest hair I have ever seen in real life: like something from a shampoo advert. I catch enough of her face to realize she looks a lot like Finn. I am just puzzling this out, thinking that he never said he had an older sister, when the young woman lifts a hand to shield her eyes and looks up. I immediately throw the curtain across my window, and in the process I lose my balance and fall off the windowsill.

At least no one is here to film me this time.

I am picking myself up and rubbing my leg where I hit it on the corner of my desk as I fell, when I hear the ominous sounds of the front door slamming and the thunder of brotherly footsteps on the stairs.

'Skye–Skye–Skye!' Harris shouts, erupting into my room like a very small and annoying volcano. 'You gotta come down. Finn's mum's here!'

Finn's *what*?

I decide I am not going to give Harris the benefit of seeing that the news interests me though.

'So?' I say, with a yawn.

'*Soooooooo*,' says Harris, his eyes gleaming. 'We've just met her outside. She has the COOLEST van! And invited us round to their house to meet her. you have to come. Our mum, I mean.' He giggles. 'I hope I get to go in the van.'

'Yes. That will be fun for you,' I say.

Harris looks puzzled. 'I told you: Mum says you have to come.'

Mum chooses that precise moment to appear in my doorway. 'Yes,' she says. 'We've all been invited. Hurry up!'

'OK, OK!' I say, flinging my book down. I get up off the floor. 'I was coming anyway,' I mutter.

Why do I have to come? And why is she in such a rush to go round?

'Wait!' Mum exclaims. She stops to check her reflection in my mirror and begins fussing with her hair and sighing. 'Oh, I look a sight. Just give me five minutes to fix my make-up.' She runs out of the room, her shabby gardening cardigan whipping up a draught as she goes.

I give a deep sigh. 'Either you're in a hurry or not.'

Harris jumps from foot to foot. 'I can't wait to see

Finn play his drum kit at last!' he says.

'We hardly need to *see* him play,' I mutter. 'It's so loud he's practically in our house when he practises anyway.'

'Come on, then,' Mum says, running back into my room. She claps her hands. 'Chop-chop!'

'All right, all right,' I say. 'Calm down.'

'It's EXCITING!' says Harris,  down the stairs. 'Finn's mum looks

Mum gives a funny whimper an   , doesn't she?'

I wonder if she is worried that she isn't such great-looking Mum Material in comparison. That makes me feel bad. I know what it's like when you feel as though you are second best.

'It's OK, Mum,' I say, giving her arm a quick squeeze. 'You're all right too, you know.'

Mum shoots me a look of bewilderment. 'Oh, Skye. That's . . . lovely,' she says and gives me a strained smile. 'Now, best behaviour everyone,' she says. She flicks her hair back and straightens her shoulders, then rings the Parkers' doorbell.

The woman from the camper van answers. She flashes the same warm smile I saw from my bedroom window and throws her arms wide as though she is about to gather all of us into a bear hug. Hundreds of skinny silver bracelets slide down over her wrist to her elbow, jingling and tinkling as they fall.

'Hi! I'm Yuki. You must be Harris and Skye – and Hellie! Rob's told me *lots* about you.' She raises an eyebrow and then laughs.

I notice Mum flinch. 'Really?' she says. Her forehead creases.

Rob has ___ wonders. 'Oh, yeah,' she says. Mum says ___ what supposed to mean?

'Mum ___ and Yuki's smile fades and her mouth shrinks to form a silent 'O' as if she realizes Mum is upset about something. The smile is soon back though.

'It's all right,' she says. 'I can sense you are feeling uncomfortable. It is understandable in the circumstances, but not at all necessary.'

'Circumstances'? What is she on about? I look from Yuki to Mum and back to Yuki again. It is like Yuki is speaking in code.

Rob appears behind Yuki and puts his hands on her shoulders, moving her to one side as though she is a bit of furniture that has been put in the wrong place.

'Hi, Hellie,' he says. 'Hi, Harris – Skye. Come on in. We can't chat with everyone standing on the doorstep like this!' He laughs, but it's the kind of fake-sounding laugh adults do when they are nervous or trying to cover up that they are annoyed. 'It's still a tip in here, I'm afraid,' he adds.

Mum mutters something and steps into the house and Harris and I troop in after her.

'Is your house similar to this?' Yuki asks. 'It must feel very familiar.' She raises one eyebrow at Mum.

'Oh, er, not really,' says Mum, avoiding Yuki's gaze. 'I mean. It's not that familiar. I mean, it's kind of similar. But I don't really know. I mean, I haven't really—'

I cut in to stop her wittering. 'It *is* pretty much the same as our house,' I say. I shoot Mum a look to try and get her to calm down. She is being really weird. She keeps patting her hair and pulling at her clothes.

'Except your house is WAY cooler,' Harris says to Rob. 'Because it's back to front!'

Rob smiles. 'You mean it's a mirror image,' he says.

'Yes!' says Mum with a tinkly laugh. 'Isn't that funny?'

What? It's not *that* funny.

Rob invites us to go through to the kitchen. I know the layout of this house every bit as well as my own, and not just because it's like Rob says: a mirror image of my house. I know it from when I used to come round and visit Mrs Robertson. It looks weird without her furniture and pictures and little knick-knacks that she used to have, covering every surface. I used to love picking up the tiny boxes and figurines she had and asking her questions

172

about them. She never told me not to touch. She loved chatting about her things. I really miss her. I asked Mum the other day if I could visit, but apparently she is not very well at the moment.

'Like I said,' Rob says, ushering us into the kitchen. 'I'm afraid it is still a bit of a tip. I don't want to unpack everything until I'm done with some of the basic DIY and painting.'

The place *is* a tip. It's crammed with unpacked boxes and the rooms look shabby and sad. There are marks on the wall where Mrs Robertson had mirrors and pictures. I am aware of how old-fashioned the decor looks. Sadness wells up in me as I think of Rob and Finn dismissing the old decor – maybe even laughing at it – and deciding what to do instead.

Is it really that easy to replace someone? Move them out, take away their things, strip off the old wallpaper, rip out the carpets: it's as if they never existed.

It makes me think of Dad. Did Mum throw out his stuff when he died? She has never once shown me anything that belonged to him: there are a few old photos to prove he existed, otherwise it's as though he never really lived. We don't have any clothes or belongings of his. Not that I know of, anyway. Maybe Mum has some squirrelled away in the loft.

My head is spinning with these thoughts so that I

don't hear the next few things Mum, Yuki and Rob say to each other as we take our places around the kitchen table.

Finn has disappeared, I realize – to his room probably (I don't blame him) – and Harris is now running after him shouting, 'Finn! Finn? Wait for me!'

'Skye, sweetie?' Mum says in a sugary tone. 'Yuki is talking to you, darling.'

I come back from my memories as though waking up from a long sleep. What's with the 'sweetie-darling' stuff all of a sudden?

'What?' I say.

'Skye!' Mum says. 'Don't be rude.'

'Don't stress: I don't offend easily,' says Yuki. 'I can see Skye is lost in thought. Perhaps this house has a special place in your heart, Skye?' She looks deep into my eyes and lays a hand on my arm.

I jump. That's a bit creepy. How does she know how I feel about this house?

'Er . . .' I don't know what to say.

'Skye was friendly with the lady who lived here before,' says Mum. 'Mrs Robertson.'

Rob nods. 'I heard she had to go into a home. Sad,' he says. 'I guess you miss her, Skye?'

I bite my lip. 'Yeah,' I say softly.

'We might visit once she's up to it,' Mum says quietly.

She puts a hand on my shoulder.

'Must be hard, getting used to new neighbours,' Rob says. 'Change can be hard at your age, eh?'

I look up at him and see he is smiling, but he looks a bit sad too. I feel a rush of warmth towards him. I hadn't thought he would understand.

'But Rob, change is a good thing,' says Yuki. 'Life is all about change. The seasons come and go, we get older, things move on.'

'Yes!' says Mum. 'That's right. We can't all stay the same forever.' She does that fake laugh again.

'Embrace change, Skye,' Yuki says, fixing me with her deep brown eyes. 'It's only when we resist it that it has the power to hurt us.'

'Mu-um . . .' Finn has reappeared, with Harris bobbing up and down beside him. 'You're not going on about all your spiritual yoga-guru stuff, are you? It's embarrassing.'

'Finn, angel,' says Yuki, stretching out an arm towards him. 'You know I don't like you calling me "Mum". That's not my name.'

'Whatever.' Finn looks as uncomfortable and grumpy as he did when I saw him from my window. I suddenly feel I understand: he doesn't like change either. His mum and dad aren't together any more and that must be really hard for him. Maybe we have more in common that I have wanted to admit.

Rob is muttering to Finn, clearly telling him to stop being so moody.

Mum glances at them and then gives that fake laugh again. 'Well. It is lovely to meet you, Yuki. I hear you're an artist.'

How does she know this? I wonder.

'What kind of art do you do?' Mum asks, pulling her chair closer.

Yuki waves her hands in a vague gesture and says, 'I try to reinterpret nature's forms through a mix of media. My work is all about perception rather than content.'

I'm not going to lie, it is pretty difficult to understand a word of what she is talking about.

Rob tuts and says, 'Yuki's a "conceptual artist" – you know, installations and whatnot – a chair in the middle of the room symbolizing death, that kind of thing.'

'Sounds *fascinating*,' says Mum. 'Must be amaaaazing having an artist in the family. I have always wanted to do something creative.'

'But you *are* an artist, Mum!' Harris pipes up. 'You did all those drawings of those naked people. They were really good. Shall I go home and get some and show them to Yuki?'

'No, Harris,' I hiss.

'How wonderful that you have a creative side. It must be such a release from your job and family commitments. I would love to see your drawings,' says Yuki.

Rob coughs loudly.

Mum looks hastily from Yuki to Rob and then ploughs on. 'And Rob tells me you have travelled all over the world,' she gushes. 'That sounds amaaaaaazing too. So, er, what brings you back here?'

Yuki smiles. 'The universe,' she says, as though it is the most obvious reason in the world.

'Oh,' says Mum.

Rob gives a tight smile and says, 'Yuki's been away for ages, haven't you? We haven't seen her for – oh, months and months.'

Yuki shrugs. 'Time is a concept I don't bother with,' she says. 'We all worry far too much about it.'

'That's *exactly* what I think,' Mum exclaims. 'I'm always saying that, aren't I, Skye?'

I am lost for words. Why is Mum being like this? She is being a total suck-up! It's like she's desperate for Yuki to like her, as though she's the loser at school with no mates who will do anything to get in with the popular crowd. She reminds me of Aubrey with the VTs. I've had enough of this. I have to get her out of here before she says anything seriously embarrassing.

I push my chair back and say, 'Talking of *time*, Mum,

don't you think it's time we went home?'

'No!' Harris whines. 'I haven't played Finn's drums yet. Can I now, Finn? Can I?'

Finn looks relieved to have a reason to leave the room. 'Sure. Come on,' he says and chases Harris, shrieking, out of the kitchen. Seconds later the familiar crashing sound of drums and cymbals can be heard.

Yuki raises an eyebrow. 'I hope that is your son playing, not mine,' she says to Mum.

Rob takes a deep breath as though he is about to say something, but Yuki jumps up before he can begin. 'Kettle's boiled!' she says. 'You may as well have a cup of tea while the boys are occupied?' she says.

Rob gives Mum a pleading look as though begging Mum to stay. Or go? I am not sure I can tell.

'Oh, yes please,' says Mum. She returns Rob's look with an expression that seems to say, 'You *bet* I am staying.'

What is going on?

'I hope you have herbal, Rob?' asks Yuki, rummaging through the cupboards.

Rob shakes his head. 'Sorry. Only builders',' he says, rocking back on his chair to pick up a box of tea bags from the work surface behind him.

'How apt,' says Yuki, taking the box from him. 'You being a builder and everything.'

'I am not a builder any more,' Rob says quietly. 'I am a construction site manager.'

'Whatever,' says Yuki. 'Just hot water with lemon for me then.' She picks up the kettle and begins making tea for us. 'I will have to rebalance my chakras after drinking unfiltered water, of course.'

Rob sucks his teeth. I don't blame him for looking peeved. Yuki is starting to annoy me.

'Ooooh,' says Mum. 'Hot water and lemon sounds so refreshing! I'll have that too.'

I wince. Can't Mum see how rude Yuki is being to Rob? I thought she and Rob were supposed to be friends and now she's siding with his ex. What has got into her?

'So what do you do, Hellie?' Yuki asks.

'Just a boring office job,' says Mum. 'What about you?'

'I am no longer tied to the world of work. I live on an ashram – when I am not travelling, that is. I prefer not to be weighed down by possessions and home-ownership.'

'Or family,' Rob mutters. I am not sure Mum hears him, she is too excited by what Yuki has just said.

'An *ashram*?' she says. Her eyes are sparkling. 'That *is* interesting. Is it very far away from here?'

'Yes,' says Yuki. 'In India.' She smiles and closes her eyes for a second, as though picturing the place in her mind. 'I decided to renounce all possessions when I left Rob, so I went to live on an ashram where I could find myself spiritually and practise yoga in the traditional way. It is the only way to truly experience peace. I couldn't do that inside the walls of a marriage and motherhood.'

'How *interesting*,' says Mum again, this time with even more feeling. She leans forward as if Yuki has all at once become the most fascinating person she has ever met.

'I seem to remember you renounced all possessions except our old camper van,' Rob says quietly. 'The one we went travelling in together.'

Yuki ignores him and says, 'You should try it, Hellie – living with nothing to tie you down. It is incredibly freeing.'

'I can imagine,' says Mum. 'So when did you make this decision?'

I have no idea what this ashram place is but I don't like the thought of losing all my possessions. I am worried that Mum is becoming fired up by the idea of being so 'free'; the mood she is in, and knowing the way she changes her mind about her hobbies, she might decide we are selling all we own right now and following Yuki on her travels.

Harris would never give up the TV, though. And you would have to kill me before I would give up my books.

'I left Rob and Finn ten years ago,' Yuki continues.

'As I say, family is a tie that constrains us. If we are to find the true meaning of our lives and remain individuals, we must break free from the bonds that hold us. In the ashram I can meditate, create, and use my own space however I wish.'

Rob gets up and collects the tea mugs, even though they are not empty. He makes a loud noise with the washing-up.

I have to say I am changing my opinion about Yuki pretty fast. She makes her life choices sound pretty selfish. Why would anyone have a kid and then decide that 'family ties them down'? I'm glad Finn's not in the room right now to hear what Yuki has just said. I can see why he is not that impressed with his mother.

My mum, on the other hand, seems more and more impressed by what she has just heard. She sits up. 'Ten years ago, you say?' she asks.

'Yes,' says Yuki. 'I had to find a way of nurturing my artistic child,' says Yuki.

'Oh, you have another child?' says Mum, her forehead wrinkling.

Rob gives a hollow laugh. 'No, Yuki means she left to discover her creative side. Not easy being an artist when you live with a *builder*,' he says.

Finn and Harris reappear as Rob is saying this. Finn looks so miserable I almost feel I should give him a hug.

I'm not surprised he's upset. It is bad enough that my dad died, but at least he didn't choose to leave us to go off and do whatever he wanted.

I hate to admit it, but I am feeling really sorry for Finn Parker.

Chapter Twenty

Mum became more and more cheerful in the days that followed. When I pointed out the fact, she went pink with pleasure and said, 'I know! Must be all this dancing. So good for the soul! In fact,' she said, as she rumba-ed around the kitchen table, 'I think I shall have to go on having lessons once the competition is over.'

This news has not exactly filled me with joy, but it is nice to see Mum so happy all the time.

I have noticed something, though: the happier Mum becomes, the quieter and less happy Harris is.

I tried asking him what was up. He said he was angry with Mum because she said he couldn't come to the dancing competition. I asked him why and he said, 'Because it's too late and she says it's past my bedtime.' I told him she was probably right. 'Maybe kids aren't even allowed to go,' I pointed out. But he just shrugged and went back to watching cartoons. He didn't even perk up when Mum announced her plans for more dancing lessons. I would have thought he would at least be thrilled that Finn would be coming round for even more babysitting.

Which, needless to say, I am not. I am going to have to talk to Mum about this. I really think I am old enough to stay home alone.

Sadly, my complaint is falling on deaf ears. It is the night of the competition and Mum is preparing snacks for us – for Finn – and going through the 'Checklist of How to Behave' yet again. As if I am not used to this after months of Finn coming round twice a week while Mum goes out.

'Please don't ask Finn round tonight,' I beg. 'It's bad enough that I go to the same school as him.'

'Skye, darling, don't be like that,' Mum says. 'Rob is so pleased Finn is spending time here. He says it has helped him settle after their move.'

'Well that's just lovely. What about me? What

about how I feel?' I say. I did feel sorry for Finn the other night, it's true, but Aubrey still isn't speaking to me, and the more Finn is round at my place, the worse things get at school.

'Why don't you invite Aubrey round as well?' Mum says. 'She could keep you company while Finn and Harris play computer games together.'

I cannot believe Mum has just said this. She just hasn't noticed a single thing about my life since she started those classes. Something inside me snaps and suddenly I am shouting at her, the words pouring out before I have a chance to check them.

'Just so you know,' I say, tears choking my voice, 'Aubrey is not my friend any more. In fact, thanks to you and your stupid dancing, I don't have *any* friends.'

Mum looks as though I have slapped her. I know I should feel guilty for blaming her, but I am so angry with her for putting her ballroom dancing before me that I plough on regardless.

'You have just been so obsessed with your classes that you haven't noticed what is going on right in front of you, have you?' I say. 'Because of you insisting we get friendly with Finn, I have lost Aubrey. And because of *that*, she has turned everyone else against me. It was the last straw when you got Rob round to unlock the bathroom to "save" me instead of helping me yourself.

In fact . . . oh no!' A shot of ice rushes through me as it dawns on me what must have really happened that day.

'What?' Mum is white-faced. Not as white-faced as I reckon I am, though.

'Aubrey did it!'

'Did what?' Mum tries to catch hold of me, but I twist away. 'Skye, darling, you are not making any sense.'

'Aubrey put the video of me falling into the loo online and now I am the laughing-stock of the whole school,' I shout.

I turn to leave the room, but Mum is too quick for me. She grabs my hand and pulls me to her. 'Darling, this is awful!' she says. She lets go of my hand, takes me gently by the shoulders and looks into my eyes, her brow crumpled with concern. 'You shouldn't have kept all this to yourself. Why didn't you tell me? Oh, you poor love!' She enfolds me in her arms and holds me tight. It would be quite a nice hug if she weren't wearing a ridiculously long necklace with a large knobbly stone on it. 'Are you sure Aubrey would do such a nasty thing?' she mumbles into my hair.

I disentangle myself. 'I know I saw her texting something when Rob broke the door down. It all makes sense. She's been trying to find a way to impress the VTs and drop me for ages. Well, she's done it now,' I say.

'Skye, this is serious,' Mum says. She tilts my chin

up to make me look into her eyes. 'I can't let this go without reporting it. Even if it is Aubrey. Bullies need to be shown they can't get away with it – you know that.'

'NO!' I yell. 'It's too late. If you go charging into school and make a complaint you will only make it worse.'

'I can't just let this go,' Mum says. She looks very anxious now. 'There must be something we can do about this. Maybe I should talk to Aubrey's mum instead?'

I shake my head. This is a disaster. Why did I open my big mouth in the first place?

Mum makes me sit down opposite her at the kitchen table. She holds my hand while she keeps talking on and on at me, repeating how serious this is and that she can't stand to see me so upset, and I know she is there for me, don't I, and surely there must be a reason for Aubrey's 'appalling behaviour', and on and on . . .

In the end I can't bear it any more. I snatch my hand away and push back my chair. Standing up, I blurt out:

'You're not listening to what I have been saying. I don't want you to charge into school *or* talk to Aubrey's mum. I have already lost my best friend, and that is bad enough.'

'Skye—'

'Listen! Aubrey isn't interested in me any more. She wants to go out with Finn, OK? And she's cross with me because he is always round here and I haven't

187

invited her round at the same time.'

'I don't understand,' Mum says. 'Would that be so bad?'

'Yes!' I cry. 'I don't WANT them to get together. It would be horrendous. It would be even worse than it is now. I would be completely left out and I couldn't stand her talking about him all the time.'

'Ah.' Mum looks more troubled than ever. I can literally see every wrinkle on her forehead. 'And – er – you have fought over this because . . . ?' She hesitates, waiting for me to fill in the blanks.

'Because he's an *idiot*!' I say, flinging my arms wide. Even as I say the words I am thinking, He's not that bad. Not as bad as Aubrey, anyway. It's not his fault she is crushing on him. Maybe I have been the idiot . . .

Mum's frown clears and she smiles. 'Oh, right!' She sounds relieved and goes on to say, 'I thought for one moment that you were going to say *you* fancied him too!'

'Mu-um! Of course I don't,' I say. 'And don't say "fancy". It's gross.'

'Well, these things happen – friends fighting over boys,' she says. 'I'm afraid romance can have a habit of getting in the way of friendships as you get older. But if you don't both fancy him, then I can't see what the problem is.'

'PLEASE don't say that word!' I say. 'You're still not

listening, anyway. I've just *told* you what the problem is.'

I am so exasperated. It is like we are talking two completely different languages.

'Aubrey likes him, OK? *Aubrey*, not me. All she wants is to follow him around like some kind of love-crazed parrot that has swallowed a whole bottle of love potion. She is not interested in me any more. She has started hanging out with the cool gang so that she can impress him and she doesn't want me holding her back. Get it?' I say. How can I get her to understand how horrible this is for me?

'Darling.' Mum keeps her voice calm and comes round to my side of the table. She puts a hand on my shoulder. I shrug it off. I wish she would stop trying to hug me. 'Please don't worry,' she says. 'It's only a phase, I promise. I'm sure Finn's not interested in Aubrey anyway, is he? She's a bit young for him. I thought it was uncool for Year 9s to mix with Year 8s?' she adds. 'Isn't that what you told me?'

'Yeah, well it turns out that this particular Year 9 doesn't seem to follow the normal rules. He likes having an eight-year-old boy as a best mate and he hangs out at school with Year 8 girls. Maybe he some kind of weird obsession with the number eight,' I add, with a dry laugh.

'Who else does he "hang out" with then?' Mum asks.

I wince at the way she says the words 'hang out', as

though she is putting quote marks around them.

'The school band. And Izzy and Livvy Vorderman,' I reply. This is not strictly true: I don't actually know that he hangs out with the VTs, but he must do, now he is in the band.

'Ah,' says Mum again. She nods. 'Those two have always been nothing but trouble. Haven't they always tried to make life difficult for you?'

'Guess so,' I say.

Mum puts her head on one side. 'You don't think maybe it was the twins who posted the video, not Aubrey? It doesn't sound like her, to be honest. I could ask the school to at least look into it—'

'NO, Mum! PLEASE.' I am crying now. I just want to go to my room. I try again to leave but Mum puts a hand on my shoulder again.

'OK, OK,' she says. 'I won't get involved. This time. But you must promise to tell me if anything like this happens again, OK?'

I nod.

'Skye?' Mum persists.

'All right, yes. I will tell you,' I mutter, brushing at my tears.

'Good.' Mum smiles, but I can tell she is only pretending. I know she feels bad for me, and that makes me feel bad too. I know she only wants to help, but I also know she can't. She can't leave it alone, either, it seems.

'As for this thing with Finn, I'm sure you and Aubrey could sort it out,' she is saying. 'Maybe if I asked her round, that would help to smooth things over. If you are alone together and on home territory – I mean, not at school and not with the twins – maybe it will be OK?'

Why can't she just drop it? I feel anger roar through me again. 'Mum, stop! I am not six. You can't go around organizing play dates for me. In any case, have you understood a word I've said? What good will it do getting her round here while *he's* here? She'll only want to talk to him, not me. Honestly, you are useless!'

'Skye . . .' Mum reaches out to me again.

But this time I really have had enough. 'Oh, just go to your stupid competition and leave me alone,' I snap. 'I'm going to my room.'

Chapter Twenty-one

I am sitting on my windowsill again. I was writing about the conversation I have just had with Mum. I have found that if I write about things that have upset me, it helps me to sort them out in my mind and it calms me down. I had just finished and was going to pick up *The Owl Service* and start reading again, when I was distracted by the sound of a door shutting. I looked out on to the street and saw Rob leaving his house and getting into his van. Then Mum came out of our house all dressed up for the dance competition in a flouncy, bouncy, over-the-top red-and-black number, and went over to talk to him. They chatted for a few seconds, then Rob got into his van and drove off. Mum glanced back briefly to our house, then got in our car and drove off as well.

It was then I realized that Yuki's camper van had gone.

Has she left for her travels again, I wonder? Maybe they have had a fight? It's a bit strange that no one mentioned it. Which makes me think: Rob always said he would stay in while Finn babysat over at ours. So why has he just gone out? Maybe he is driving after Yuki to get her to come back?

Oh well, I guess he and Mum were chatting just before he left, so Mum knows he's gone out. Why should I care? It's not as if Rob has ever come round to check on us while Mum's dancing, in any case.

There is a vague thought niggling at the back of my mind, though. I can't pin it down. It's like a lost memory or a nagging reminder to do something I have forgotten about. I don't think I can go back to reading now. I feel all fidgety and my bum is going numb, sitting up here. I am going downstairs to grab a snack before Finn eats them all.

I walk past the sitting-room door, expecting to hear the usual electronic pinging and whizzing from the TV screen, but instead it is quiet and I hear the occasional murmur of voices, Harris's higher voice slightly louder than Finn's deep mumble.

'. . . says I can't any more,' Harris is saying.

I don't catch exactly what he is talking about, but he sounds really miserable. Is he still upset about not going to the competition? Is Finn being mean to him? I immediately tense up: if Finn has done something to upset my little brother, he is going to have me to reckon with. I make a move to enter the room and tell Finn to leave Harris alone, then I hear Finn say:

'Hey, buddy, don't cry. People can be idiots, you just have to ignore them.'

Harris sniffs, 'I can't.'

What are they talking about? I squint through the gap in the door jamb and see Finn scoot over to Harris's side of the sofa and give him a quick one-armed hug. 'Listen, d'you want me to have a word? I could pretend I am your big brother?' he says.

Big *brother*? A cold spear of outrage shoots through me. Harris doesn't need a big brother! He's got me – his big sister. If he is upset about something at school, he should be telling me.

I am fizzing with outrage now, but don't know how to

come in on the conversation without making it obvious I have been snooping.

'I don't want to go to school tomorrow,' says Harris.

Finn sighs. 'Shall I tell you a secret?' he says. 'Nor do I.'

Am I hearing this right? Mr Popular, not want to go to school? I can't believe that. Maybe it is because he hasn't achieved entire world domination with his popularity or something . . .

Finn is speaking again. 'Ever since everyone found out I can't actually play the drums, it's been hell.'

'What do you mean, you can't play? Are the drums broken?' Harris says. 'I think you are an awesome drummer,' he adds.

Hero-worship. Urgh.

Finn sighs again. 'No, nothing's broken. I'm *not* good, not good enough, anyway, that's the point. Dad bought me the drums as a bribe for moving here. I started having lessons just before we moved. I was doing OK, not great or anything. And I loved it . . . but then Mum arrived and since then, she's been on and on at me about how the drums 'affect our *shanti*', and that I should choose a calmer instrument like the flute or something, so I stopped playing.' His voice is laced with bitterness now.

'What is "shanty"?' asks Harris.

'It means "inner peace",' Finn snorts. 'The only

thing that was upsetting me was having Mum around,' he adds.

'Why did your dad bribe you to move? Don't you like it here?' Harris asks. I can hear the confusion in his high-pitched voice. It makes me realize how young he still is. I feel funny. Like I want to run in there and give him a huge bear hug and tell him everything's going to be all right.

Finn hesitates. 'I do . . . It's just . . .' He pauses again. Then says, in a rush: 'I didn't want to move. I had mates where we lived before. I liked my room, my school – everything,' he adds. 'I didn't want anything to change. I don't like change. I have never liked it. Maybe it's cos of Mum leaving. I dunno.' His voice is quieter now. Sullen. And sad.

I swallow. I shouldn't be listening to this. Finn would hate it if he knew I was eavesdropping on him getting all deep-and-meaningful with Harris.

Poor Finn, though. His mum left him when he was four, he had to move here and didn't want to, and things aren't working out for him at school. I can hardly stay mad at him now I know all this, can I?

Still, it doesn't help me and my situation, I remind myself. I still don't have any friends either, and Finn hasn't exactly done anything to help that. Oh boy, I am as confused as Harris now.

I tune back into the boys' conversation.

'Dad had to move for his work,' Finn is saying, 'and I couldn't go and live with Mum because she is always travelling around. She needs to be "free to express herself",' he adds. His voice has a sharp, bitter edge to it. 'In other words, she doesn't want me hanging around and getting in the way . . . I sometimes wish I had a mum like yours.'

I peep through the crack of open door and see Harris snuggle his head into the crook of Finn's shoulder. 'You can pretend she's your mum if you like,' he says softly.

I am feeling really bad now. I should turn around and creep away, but I can't.

'Thanks, buddy,' Finn says with a soft smile. 'Anyway, Dad said the move would be good for us and when I complained he promised he would get me some drums and some lessons, cos he knows I have always wanted to learn. He got them before we moved and I started the lessons and I loved it, so I thought, maybe, I don't know, maybe things would be OK. And then I met the guys in the band at school and that was cool at first—'

'The Warthogs?' says Harris.

I can tell he is proud of himself for knowing about this.

'Yeah,' says Finn, 'The Hogs.' He pauses. 'Your sister's mate, Aubrey, told me she could get me into the band. I guess maybe Skye had told her I played the drums.'

'Or Aubrey might have seen you bringing your drums into your house when you moved in. She and Skye were spying on you that day,' says Harris, his voice full of glee.

Thanks, little bro!

Finn ignores Harris's last comment and goes on, 'Anyway, the trouble was, I had only just started having lessons. I got carried away with the idea of being in the band and told them that I could play anything. But then when they said they really did want me, I was too embarrassed to tell them that I had only had a few lessons. I kept making up excuses not to come to sessions. I started practising like mad at home, hoping I would get good enough to go soon, but then Mum turned up . . .'

'What's *her* problem?' Harris asks.

I smile at him trying to sound cool.

'Oh, all her usual stuff,' Finn says, that edge back in his voice. 'Rock music is "disturbing" and "messes with my aura". She says I need to learn to "be still". I tried ignoring her at first and playing anyway – just to annoy her!'

'Yeah!' says Harris.

'But I can't explain – she just gets to me. Argh!' There is a noise as though Finn is smacking his hand down on the table. 'She just doesn't *understand* how important it is to me, being in The Hogs.' He sounds really angry now. 'I can't keep avoiding going to the sessions without an explanation, but if I turn up now and try to play, they'll see how rubbish I am. And then I will have stuffed up everything for the band because they really need a drummer soon, otherwise they won't be able to play at the half-term gig. The posters are already up all around the school, thanks to Aubrey and her evil twin friends. They think they are like some kind of groupies of something. They just won't leave it alone: following me around the whole time, begging me to get them in The Hogs as backing singers or whatever. I bet your sister is probably in on it as well. She and Aubrey are, like, glued together, aren't they?'

I wish.

'Argh!' Finn cries again. I hear him get up and start pacing the room. 'I wish Mum hadn't come to stay,' he says. 'At least she's gone now. That's what she does, though: turns up without letting us know and disappears just as quickly.' I hear the smacking sound again.

'She seemed nice . . .' Harris says.

'Oh, come ON!' says Finn, his voice rising. 'You think so? What about her camper van? It is *sooo* embarrassing. She was going to take me to school in it. I would NEVER be allowed to forget it if she did. I ended up having the mickey taken at my last school because of her.'

Wow. He really is fed up with Yuki. I have to admit she did make some pretty snidey comments when we were round there, but I also thought she was kind of exotic. And the van was cool. I would love it if Mum took me to school in a van like that.

She does sound mean, though, saying those things about Finn's drumming. I would be beside myself if my mum announced that I shouldn't read so much – that it was bad for my 'aura', or whatever. I guess the drumming means as much to Finn as reading and writing does to me.

Maybe my mum is not so bad after all. She doesn't tell me what I can and can't do. And she is always here for me.

Should I go in and say something . . . ?

As I am mulling this over and wondering what I would say, Pongo comes out of the kitchen to find me. He starts whining, like he needs to go out for a pee.

'Shh, boy,' I say, creeping away from the door. I don't want Finn and Harris to come out and find me listening in on them.

'So, spying on me again, were you?'

Too late. Finn has opened the door and caught me loitering. His face is dark with fury.

'I . . .' I can hardly deny that I was eavesdropping, but I don't know what to say.

'You and your little friends – it's either you or Aubrey or those toxic twins, on my back all the time,' Finn spits. 'It's like you're determined to wreck my chances at having any friends in this place.'

My throat has gone dry. I can't think of anything to say back. I turn away from him. He might be angry with Yuki, but there is no need to take it out on me. I head to the kitchen.

'Yeah, that's right, run away,' Finn says. 'You never have the guts to face up to anything.'

How dare he!

I spin around, squaring up to him. '*I* haven't got the guts?' I repeat. I am dimly aware of Harris behind Finn, hovering in the doorway to the sitting room, but I am not going to let Finn get away with that last comment. 'What about you and your little sob story about the band?' I say. 'Seems like *you* haven't got the guts to tell anyone what you're really like.'

The words burst out of me before I can think of what I am saying. I know I am being mean, and the look on Finn's face makes me regret what I have just said.

His jaw is tight. He is all pent-up anger and energy, like a coiled spring. All he says is, 'I can't.'

Then it is as though someone has pulled a plug on my emotions. I don't want to fight any more. I have lost my best friend already, everyone at school is laughing at me, even Mum doesn't seem to understand me. I have just heard Finn pretty much admit to Harris that he feels the same and I have heard Harris say that he doesn't want to go to school, so there is clearly something going on with him too. Which means I have not been a good big sister, as I have not been there for him.

I feel all the irritation and anger of the past few weeks drain away from me and in its place is a dragging tired sensation.

'Finn,' I say. 'I am sorry I was eavesdropping just then—'

'Spying,' he says.

'Whatever,' I say. 'I *am* sorry. It's just that I thought you were cool with everyone at school. I thought everyone loved you. In fact I have been jealous. Which probably means I have been a dork. No wonder Aubrey doesn't want to hang out with me any more . . .' I take a deep breath. 'Now I know how you really feel, maybe I can help?'

'Thanks, but I think I've had enough of people trying to help,' Finn says, turning away.

'Maybe we should try to work things out,' I say. 'It is pretty harsh, you coming round here all the time and us not talking.'

Finn's shoulders drop when I say that, as though he too has given up the fight. 'Guess,' he says. He looks me in the eye then and says, 'I do like coming round here a lot, you know. It's nice feeling part of a normal family.'

'NORMAL?' I say. 'You have got to be joking!'

We both start laughing and it feels great to be like this, relaxing, not bickering.

'Hey, we should do something all together while Mum's out,' I say. 'Watch a movie?'

Finn nods.

'I'll ask Harris what he wants to watch,' I say. 'Harris!' I shout. 'Want to watch a film?' When he doesn't answer I scoot past Finn and go out into the hall. 'Harris?' I say again.

Then I see something that knocks the breath from my lungs.

The front door is open.

Harris has gone.

Chapter Twenty-two

'Harris? HARRIS! . . . Finn! You've got to help me.'

Finn puts his hand on my shoulder and says, 'Don't panic. I'll look outside, you check inside in case he's just playing a trick on us.'

'Really?'

Finn gives me a small smile. I know he is only trying to make me feel better. 'You mustn't immediately assume the worst.'

But that is just what I *am* assuming. Harris was upset. I heard him talking to Finn. He was upset and now he has run away, and it is all my fault because I have been a rubbish sister.

My heart is scampering in time with my feet as I race around the house, shouting for my brother, looking in every room, even in wardrobes, the shower, under the bed . . .

My chest is tight. Where has he got to?

'Where ARE you, Harris? If this *is* a trick, like Finn says, you are so going to regret this.'

WHERE IS MY LITTLE BROTHER?

'Who is going to regret what?' says a voice.

I look up and see the strangest vision. For a moment I think I must be hallucinating. A creature is standing in the open front doorway. It's a girl. I think. She has dark curly hair pinned up on top of her head. She is wearing a kind of medieval wench's outfit: a cream blouse under a laced bodice with a very full brown skirt. And her feet are bare. And enormous. And hairy!

'Er, hi?' I say.

'Your mum called. Said it was important I come round right away. Unfortunately it was a Ring Night at our place. The house is crawling with elves and hobbits. I couldn't get into my room to change. So, where's your mum and why are you standing in the hall with the front door open, talking to yourself?'

'Aubrey?' I say.

'The one and only,' she says, bowing.

I am stunned. Aubrey is unbelievable. She has humiliated me in front of the whole school and now she turns up as though everything is OK between us? And that outfit! This really is taking things to a whole new level. Does she seriously think Finn is going to go for her dressed like that?

'Just go away, Aubrey,' I say. 'We don't need you. We've got a crisis on our hands.'

'What?' Aubrey frowns.

'She's right,' says a voice from behind her.

Aubrey turns to see Finn. She shrieks, pulls her wig off and throws it towards me. It lands on Gollum, who has chosen that moment to come down the stairs. She hisses and scoots past Aubrey and Finn into the street, still wearing the wig.

Finn pulls a face. 'Nice one, Hobbit,' he says. 'Don't suppose you have Gandalf with you? We could do with some magic right about now.'

'I know I look utterly mental. Blame Mum,' Aubrey babbles. She shuffles along to the coat rack and tries to pull one of Mum's coats over her hairy feet to hide them. 'She insisted I dress up and join in. It's not like I had anything else to do, anyway, what with my best friend abandoning me and everything,' she says, shooting daggers at me.

'Oh shut up and go back to The Shire,' I shout. 'Life isn't all about you, Aubrey Stevens. I have lost my little brother, OK? He's gone missing and I can't waste time standing here talking to a hairy-footed freak show.' A sob erupts from me.

Finn looks horrified. 'Don't cry,' he says. Then he turns to Aubrey and seems to grow a couple of inches.

He fixes her with a stern look and says, 'I think you should leave. Skye and I have to think about how to find Harris.'

Aubrey's expression turns to shock as she realizes this *is* a proper crisis situation after all. 'I'll help,' she says. 'Just tell me what to do.'

I turn to Finn. 'I'm so worried about him,' I whisper.

'Shh, it's OK,' says Finn, patting my arm. 'I'm sure we'll find him. He can't have got far. Like you said, we can't waste any more time. We need to search the streets. And I need to tell you something . . .' He looks guilty.

'What?' I say, swiping at a hot tear on my face. What does he know that I don't?

'I'll tell you on the way,' says Finn, jumping to his feet. 'Come on.' He sounds decisive, in control. I am grateful. I feel anything but.

Aubrey leans in to me. 'So, are you two going out, then?' she says under her breath. 'Cos, you know, if you are, that's OK. I know I've been a bit—'

'No!' I say through gritted teeth. 'We are not! And actually could you just shut up? Cos right now I don't want to talk to you. I just want to find Harris.'

Aubrey gasps.

I turn away from her. I don't want to give her the satisfaction of seeing any more tears. I swallow hard.

Finn is calling for Pongo. The dog charges out of

the kitchen, panting with excitement at the thought of a walk.

'It would be good to take Pongo. If anyone can find him, Pongo can,' Finn explains. 'And when we find Harris, it will cheer him up to see his dog,' he adds, smiling.

It dawns on me that Finn knows Harris pretty well after all the time they have spent together. My stomach lurches with guilt as I think of how I have judged him and how moody I have been.

'What were you going to tell me? Is it about Harris?' I ask, as I shut the door behind us.

Finn crouches down and concentrates on getting Pongo's lead on. 'It's not important now. I'll tell you later,' he says, keeping his voice low. He stands up, handing me the lead.

'OK,' he says, looking at me and Aubrey. 'Where shall we go first? Split up or stay together?'

'Stay together,' says Aubrey.

I push away the thought that she *would* say that. I have to focus on finding Harris.

'Yeah,' I say. 'Let's start together, anyway. He can't have got that far.'

I am not sure I believe myself. What if someone's picked him up? He knows not to go with strangers, though. But what if . . . ?

I make myself concentrate on listening to Finn. He suddenly seems a lot more older and serious than I have ever seen him before.

We start by walking up and down our street, calling for Harris. Pongo strains to get ahead of us, keen to be let off and have a run around.

There is no sign of Harris in anyone's garden, and I am pretty sure he wouldn't be in anyone's house. He has no friends in the street other than Finn.

'What about the park?' says Aubrey.

I go cold as I think of him all alone in the park. The evenings are lighter now, but still. He is only eight.

'Good idea,' says Finn. 'Then maybe split up once we get there? Harris likes the swings . . .'

I know that he would never go to the swings on his own, though. He has never been anywhere on his own before.

'OK,' I croak.

Pongo starts pulling harder on the lead. He has just seen a cat and he's desperate to chase it.

'Pongo, heel!' I shout. It is no good, he is stronger than me and I am being dragged towards the cat. I am already thinking that bringing Pongo with us was not such a great idea after all. I am thinking of telling Finn that I will take Pongo back. Then I see something that makes me gasp.

'Finn!'

He spins round. 'What? What's the matter?'

I point to the fence at the end of our road.

My finger is trembling. 'It's Harris's blanket,' I whisper.

Finn picks it up and inspects it. 'This is what he's been using as a cape, right?' he says. 'For his dancing routines?'

I nod. 'He's been twirling it around his head, pretending to do the tango.'

'How cute!' Aubrey coos. 'I didn't know your brother was into dancing!'

I turn on her. 'Yeah, well, you don't know a lot about us these days, do you? Too busy being a suck-up with the Voldemort Twins and stalking The Hogs.'

'Oh shut up,' Aubrey sneers. 'You haven't exactly been the best friend in the world either.'

Finn's mouth has twisted into a grim expression. 'Will *both* you guys shut up for a second? We need to focus on Harris.'

'Sorry.' I am brought up short. He is right. I feel ashamed for letting my own silly little problems get in the way. I glance at Aubrey. She is shuffling her hobbity feet and looking pretty awkward too.

Finn isn't concerned with us any more. He is looking up and the down the main road which leads from the end of our cul-de-sac to the park. 'Let's head for the park first,' he says, and starts jogging.

He has long legs and it is tricky keeping up with him, even with Pongo pulling me along. Still, I am doing better than Aubrey: she hasn't got a chance with those massive hobbit feet.

My breath starts to catch in my chest, both because I'm running and because panic is squeezing my heart and making my brain race with bad thoughts of what could have happened to Harris. What did Finn want to say earlier? I have to know.

I put on a spurt and catch up with him. 'Tell me what you were going to say back there,' I say, panting.

Finn slows down a notch. 'I'm guessing you heard what Harris and I were talking about? When you were listening in?'

I bristle. 'I was NOT listening—'

Finn cuts me off. 'Whatever. It doesn't matter. The trouble is, I – I am not sure Harris would be happy me telling you, but I kind of think I have no choice now . . .'

'Telling me what?'

Finn looks sideways at me. 'I'm worried Harris has done something stupid.'

I grab his arm to slow him down. 'Why? What's the matter? What did Harris tell you?' I gabble. 'You said you were going to tell me something—'

'OK, OK!' Finn says. He slows to a walk again and shakes my hand off. 'He's being bullied,' he mutters, looking at his feet.

'WHAT?' I shout. My stomach clenches. I *knew* he was unhappy. But I can't think straight. Before I know it, I am taking my guilt out on Finn. 'My little brother is being bullied and he told *you* and not me? And now he's disappeared and you didn't think to tell me this earlier?'

Aubrey has caught up at last. She is too out of breath to speak.

Finn shoots me a look of irritation. 'I'm telling you now, aren't I?' he says. 'He's being bullied because of his dancing. He joined a class at school, even though he was the only boy. So now the other boys are calling him a freak and generally being idiots about it.' He sighs. 'I tried telling him he should ignore them – thing is, he says he didn't care at first when they just called him names and stuff, but recently they've taken money from him and he says they've made his friends turn against him too.'

I feel sick. How can I not have known this about my own brother? I am a terrible, terrible sister.

'S-so is this why he's been talking to you so much?' I ask.

Finn nods. 'I'm sorry, Skye,' he says. 'He made me promise not to tell you.' He looks at Aubrey. 'You OK to carry on?' he asks. 'I think we should keep going to the park. I just have a hunch.'

'OK,' I say.

Aubrey nods, still clearly out of breath.

Pongo is keen to get going and helps me along by pulling ahead. I scan all around me for signs of Harris as I jog along. He can't have run away. He can't have!

Cars occasionally speed past us. The horrible thought that he might have been taken by someone – bundled into a car – flashes in front of my eyes. I can hear my blood pounding in my ears as I run faster. I should slow down, look more carefully, but I can't stop running now. I look into people's gardens and down the side alleys where people keep their wheelie bins. At one point, up ahead, I see what I think is a small hunched person on the side of the road. Is it my brother? Has he been hit by a car?

'Harris!' I scream as I career towards it. Pongo lets out a yelp. His ears are flat as we both speed ahead of the others.

Finn runs faster too and overtakes me again. When I reach him he is bent over double in front of the person, wheezing and panting.

'Is it . . . ?'

Finn is shaking his head. He takes a step away and points. 'Not him.'

It's one of those charity bags, spilling old, unwanted clothes into the road, that's all. The relief brings more tears.

'I can't run any more,' I sob.

Finn stands upright. 'Come on, into the park. We're nearly there.'

We hurry around the corner of the road that the park is on. I can see the gates up ahead. There is no one in sight.

Aubrey has stayed quiet since Finn told me about Harris being bullied. I wonder if she is feeling guilty too, for stirring up trouble when things were going wrong in my life.

I am about to say something when Finn exclaims, 'Hey!'

I look at him and see he is pointing to the left of the park gates, where the road goes on to the shops. A small figure is dragging his feet, ambling towards us, his head down.

'Harris? HARRIS! Is that you?' Finn shouts.

The figure stops in its tracks and then throws its arms in the air and starts running in our direction.

'Harris!' Aubrey and I yell his name together.

Pongo immediately jerks his lead out of my hand

and goes racing ahead, catching up with Harris before I get a chance to regain my balance, and jumping up at him, licking him all over his face.

Finn gets to him before we do and grabs him in a friendly headlock, ruffling his hair.

I get to them just as Harris is saying, 'I dropped Bop-Bop somewhere – have you seen it?'

'This manky old thing?' I say, holding the blanket out to him.

I don't know whether to laugh or cry or get angry with my little brother. I decide on none of the above and throw my arms around him instead, which means I end up in an awkward tangle with him and Finn, who is still holding on to Harris too.

We pull apart, laughing and panting, out of breath and tangled up in Pongo's lead.

'You had us seriously worried, Harris,' says Finn. 'We thought you'd run away.'

Harris takes Pongo's lead and fiddles with it, looking sheepish. 'I'm sorry. You scared me when you started fighting, so I went to find Mum.'

'Oh, Harris! *I'm* the one who should be sorry. Finn has told me all about what's been going on at school. I've been a rubbish sister,' I say.

Harris gives a small smile and says, ''S'all right.'

Finn pats him on the shoulder. 'Come on,

buddy. Let's get you home.'

'No,' says Harris. 'I have to find Mum. She wasn't there.'

'What do you mean?' I ask. I shoot a glance at Finn. He shrugs.

'I just told you: I went to find her. I wanted to watch her in the competition, remember? I know she said I wouldn't be allowed, but I was upset and I wanted to see her. But when I got to the town hall, she wasn't there. There *was* a competition,' he adds, looking puzzled, 'but Mum wasn't in it. I asked one of the grown-ups who was organizing it and they said Mum hadn't been to any classes for weeks.'

My stomach falls away. 'What?' I say.

'Come on, Harris,' Finn says, his tone disbelieving. 'Your mum wouldn't lie to you.'

'Yeah,' says Aubrey. 'Are you sure you went to the right place?'

Harris glances at Aubrey's feet, then gives her an odd look, and nods.

'It's OK, it's only me, Aubrey,' she says. 'I had to dress up like this because—'

'We haven't got time for that,' Finn cuts in. 'Harris is upset, aren't you, buddy?' He puts an arm around Harris, whose eyes have filled with tears.

He nods again. 'I know I went to the right place.

Look.' He hands me a crumpled piece of paper. 'I found this in her room ages ago.'

I take it and unfold it, smoothing the creases with my fingers. It is a flyer for the ballroom-dancing competition. 'Yup, it says it's at the town hall and it's the same time that Mum mentioned.' I look up at Finn and Aubrey. 'So where is she?'

Finn takes a deep breath. 'Only your mum knows the answer to that question. I think we had better go back and wait for her.' He gently points Harris and Pongo in the direction of home and they walk on together.

Then Aubrey turns to me and says something unbelievable.

'Maybe she's on a date.'

'*What?*' I snarl.

Aubrey takes a faltering step back, tripping slightly over her stupid feet. 'I – I said, "Maybe she's on a date." Well, she did say she needed to get out and "meet people", didn't she? Maybe she met someone at the class and they've been dating in secret – so as not to upset you and Harris.' The last part comes out in a rush as I take a menacing step towards her.

'Shut up!' I say. I try to keep my voice level. I have already frightened Harris once this evening, I don't want him to turn around and see me fighting with my ex-best friend. I wait a beat until I am sure Harris and Finn are out of earshot, then I look Aubrey up and down.

'Just shut up,' I repeat. 'Everything you do and say these days is designed to hurt or humiliate me, isn't it?'

'What?' Aubrey frowns.

'Don't be all "innocent face" with me,' I say. 'You and I both know you posted that video of me falling in the loo. Mum was going to report you, you know. I wish I'd let her now.'

Aubrey's jaw drops. 'I –I . . .' For once in her life she seems to have lost the power of speech. I take advantage of this unusual state to power on, pointing at the clothes she is wearing, 'Look at you! I should be taking a video of you right now to get my own back. Except I won't because the difference between me and you is, *I* am not a bully.' I pause while Aubrey gasps. 'Yes. That's right. What you did was horrible. And now you have to turn up tonight of all nights after weeks of ignoring me. I wish you'd just go back to your new best friends and leave me alone.'

Aubrey has gone red. She flicks her eyes ahead to Finn, but he and Harris are deep in conversation and well ahead of us now. He is probably desperate to get away from us – from Hobbit-Girl Aubrey, anyway – and I don't blame him.

'Skye – I . . . I'm so sorry,' she whispers. She takes a step towards me, stumbling in her stupid Hobbit feet.

I wave a hand at her. 'Don't,' I say.

'Please, Skye. I didn't think. I didn't mean to really hurt you. I know I've been an idiot. Can you forgive me?' Her tone is pleading, her face twists as though she is going to cry. 'I came tonight because I wanted to see you. I just kind of . . . miss you,' she goes on, her voice rising in pitch as she goes on in a rush, 'and you don't ever have your phone on any more and your mum texted and told me to come and make things up with you. I know she's really angry with me. Oh, Skye, I've messed everything up, haven't I?'

I shrug. I am trying to remain careless, but really I am confused. Mum told her to come round? She promised she wouldn't get involved!

Aubrey blinks and clears her throat, pulling herself together. 'In any case,' she says, forcing a grin, 'I needed to get out of the house. I mean, elves and hobbits. Soooo uncool.'

I know what she is doing now: trying to make me laugh. I can feel myself giving in to her, wanting us to be friends again. But I can't let her win me over that easily. Not after everything she's done.

'Too right,' I say, eyeing her ridiculous outfit. 'And what do you mean, *Mum* texted you?' I ask. 'How does she even know your number? Aubrey, what is going on? Is this yet another plan to get a date with Finn? Cos I don't think it's working.' All the time I am saying this, a tiny voice in the back of my head is saying, *She missed you! And she said she was sorry: why can't you just focus on that?*

Aubrey is looking at me strangely. Her eyes have gone glassy and her mouth is trembling. I think she is about to shout at me, or say something really cutting, like the VTs would.

'I felt so bad when I got your mum's text,' she says. She fishes her phone out from the pocket of her hobbity-brown skirt and shows me, 'See? She is obviously worried about you and it's all my fault!' she says, her voice rising as tears spill on to the front of her blouse.

I read the text in disbelief. I can see from the time it was sent that Mum must have written it just after I shouted at her. I have hardly used my phone at all these past few weeks. I can't even remember the last time I saw it: there's been no point in having it on since Aubrey and I stopped talking. Mum must have taken it to get Aubrey's number.

'Skye, you have to believe me. It wasn't my idea, posting that video,' Aubrey is saying. 'It was Izzy and Livvy. They are so mean! And I've taken it down now anyway, I promise. As soon as I got your mum's text I realised I had been as mean as the VTs, so I went and deleted it.' She takes a deep, hiccupy breath and bites her lip. 'They'll have put photos of *me* on the internet by now. I know what you are going to say: "I told you so",' she says. 'I shouldn't have gone off with them and been horrible to you.' Then she flings her arms around me and says, 'Please forgive me, Skye, I really *have* missed you so much!'

I am shocked. Aubrey never blubs like this. She just styles it out. Have the VTs really got to her too?

Is this an act? Is she really crying? *Should* I tell her 'I told you so'? Should I ask her about these photos? Challenge her to find out if she is telling the truth this time?

Then I notice something. Something which makes me realize that Aubrey is not faking any of this.

She has her friendship bracelet back on.

I can't add insult to injury. The VTs have done enough damage. I am not going to be like them.

'I've missed you too,' I croak, returning Aubrey's hug.

We stand in the middle of the pavement, clinging to each other like a pair of sobbing limpets until I say, 'I need to get back. I have to find out where Mum is. You coming?'

Aubrey pulls away. 'Yes,' she says, smiling through her tears. 'Of course. I've been a dweeb, but I am back from Dweebville now. I'm here for you.' She holds up the wrist with the friendship bracelet on. 'BFF?' she says.

I hold my bracelet up to hers. 'BFF,' I say, grinning. Boy, does it feel good to be friends again. 'But can you promise me something?' I ask.

'Anything.'

'Take that costume off and wear something of mine the minute we get back?' I say. 'Those feet are grossing me out.'

Aubrey laughs. 'You bet!'

Chapter Twenty-three

Finn, Harris, Aubrey and I sit on the sofa in a line. Harris is sitting squarely between Aubrey and Finn. Aubrey keeps stealing glances at Finn when she thinks he isn't looking. We are watching a film and waiting for Mum to come home.

Aubrey changed into a pair of my jeans and one of my T-shirts as soon as we got in. She started to moan that I didn't have anything cool to wear, but she soon shut up when I snapped that she could always stay as a hobbit if she thought Finn would be more likely to have a crush on her dressed like that.

Harris said wanted to make popcorn, so Finn put some on for him. He put extra sugar on top, saying it was 'good for shock', and winked at Harris. He really does get on well with my little brother. I would feel annoyed, only it is so good to have Harris back safe and sound, I realize I don't care. In any case,

I am worried sick about Mum.

Only Harris is eating the popcorn. We are all very subdued and I don't think any of us except Harris are actually watching the film. I steal a look at Finn and Aubrey, and wonder if the same thoughts are bouncing around their brain the way they are around mine: How could Mum lie? Where has she been? Is she coming back? Why isn't she answering her phone?

When we hear the key in the front door, we all jump.

'Mum!' Harris shouts, running to greet her.

I feel sick. How do you confront your mum about the fact you know she has not been telling the truth? And what if Aubrey's comment about Mum having met someone is true?

I hear Mum laughing and chatting as she rattles her key in the lock. She has someone with her. I hear a deeper mumble: a man's voice. So Aubrey's hunch was right. She *has* been out on a date without telling us. How long has this been going on? If she is bringing him home she must be serious about him. Maybe she's decided that the time has come for us to meet him. I can't handle this. Get me out of here!

The door closes and I hear Mum cooing over Harris in the hall.

I look at Finn and Aubrey. They look back at me. If only I had some Floo Powder. I would step into the fireplace, taking the others with me, and vanish straight up the chimney.

We stand up as one. I feel squashed, like a jack-in-the-box shut up tight and ready to burst with questions the minute Mum walks in. Who is the man? Do I already know him? What will I say? What will he be like?

'Hello!' Mum is standing in the doorway, holding Harris's hand, looking in at us all standing in a line.

She is still wearing the red-and-black outfit she had on when she apparently went to the 'competition'. So what *has* she been doing? 'How lovely,' she is saying. 'A welcome committee. Harris is up late, isn't he? And Aubrey's here too! It's lovely to see you. We haven't seen you for ages!' she exclaims.

Like she didn't have anything to do with Aubrey coming round. Wow. She really *is* good at lying.

'Rob, are you coming in?' Mum calls back into the hall.

Rob?

'Hi, guys.' Rob appears in the doorway behind Mum. 'You ready to come home, Finn?'

Rob. As in Finn's dad Rob. So not a date. So . . .

Mum, Harris and Rob come into the room and everyone begins talking at once.

'Where have you been?' I say. 'Harris went to find you.'

'I was worried about you, Mum!' Harris whines.

'We know you weren't at the competition,' says Aubrey. I nudge her to stay out of this.

'Were you together?' Finn asks. His voice is steady and calm, but it sends a chill through me.

Everyone stops talking as suddenly as they began.

No one says anything for what seems like an age.

Mum looks at Rob, and Rob looks away.

Then Mum laughs and says, 'What a funny thing to say!' Her face is redder than I have ever seen it. 'Of course we were together – on the doorstep – just now. Rob saw me coming back from the competition and . . . er, well, ha ha! Now I'm back, Finn can go home, can't he? So Rob came in with me to get him. Like he sometimes does. And now he's here. With me.'

Mum is babbling. She gives another laugh – more uncertain this time. I scrutinize her face. She is nervous. But why?

Rob shuffles his feet and looks everywhere but at me and Finn.

'Hellie,' he says. 'Don't you think it's about time we . . . ?'

'About time you what?' says Finn. He draws his shoulders back and juts his chin out, as though he is challenging his dad. I don't dare look at Aubrey in case she is swooning or something.

Rob and Mum exchange glances. They look guilty. As though they have been caught doing something they shouldn't. As though . . . Hang on a minute!

'Hellie?' Rob says again.

I feel as though I am in a lift: I have gone right up to the top floor of the tallest skyscraper and then someone has cut the cords, sending me plummeting down the shaft.

They aren't . . . ? They're not . . . ?

Rob clears his throat. 'Let's all sit down,' he says. He puts a hand on Mum's shoulder.

'Yes,' says Mum. 'Good idea. We . . . er, we should probably have a chat.'

By now it is pretty obvious, even to me, what they are about to say. I can't look anyone in the eye. I am terrified of looking at Mum and I don't want to think about what is going through Finn's mind. As for Aubrey . . . I'm just glad the VTs aren't in the wings, ready to witness this. Think of the gossip that would be going around school first thing on Monday morning!

Skye's mum is going out with Finn's dad!

Kill. Me. Now.

The Last Chapter in the

Mortifying life

~~Chronicles~~ of Skye Green (or is it...?)

As Winnie-the-Pooh (greatest philosopher of all time) says: 'Life is a journey to be experienced, not a problem to be solved.'

When I said this to Finn, he pulled a face and said, 'It sounds like the kind of thing Mum - I mean Yuki - would say.'

Maybe, but Winnie-the-Pooh said it first. And it's true: I have spent the last few weeks trying to solve The Parent Problem, The Aubrey Problem and The Finn Problem, when there were actually much bigger things going on right under my nose that I didn't see at all.

Mum and Rob sheepishly told us that they had in fact been going out for months. Mum had been to a couple of dance classes, and then gave up once Rob asked her on a date.

'We didn't think we should tell you until we were sure it would work out,' Mum told us the night Harris went missing.

'Yes,' said Rob. 'We knew it would be weird for you, so we wanted to be certain. The best way of keeping it a secret was to use the cover of the dance lessons for our dates,' he said.

Finn and I were not exactly over the moon about the fact our parents had been lying to us. Plus, it was weird, however they explained it. But Harris was thrilled at the news. 'This means you kind of ARE like my big brother!' he cried, much to my annoyance.

I got over that feeling pretty quickly, though, when Finn helped Harris stand up to the bullies. Turns out all you need to scare a load of eight-year-olds into being nice to you is to get your almost six-foot-tall fourteen-year-old friend to come and pick you up from school one day.

'I didn't even have to say that Finn would sort them out if they were mean to me again,' Harris said, bursting with pride. 'They just took one look at him and they knew they couldn't mess with me.'

I had to smile at that. It was a pretty cool thing for Finn to do.

He also helped me and Aubrey out with the VTs. The main reason she had fallen out with them was that they had found photos of her and her family at the last HobbitCon and had sent them whizzing around the school. They were livid with her when The Hogs wouldn't let them be backing singers and blamed her for 'keeping Finn to herself'. Finn stepped in and told them to back off: otherwise there would be photos of *them* in matching pink dresses with bows in their hair going round the school. Apparently their mum had entered them for a 'Twins' Beauty Contest' when they were three, and Finn had found the photos on the web by just googling them. It was their turn to be mortified, so they agreed to keep their mouths shut and leave me and Aubrey alone.

In return, I made Aubrey go and explain to The Hogs that Finn wasn't ready to be their drummer. Even that worked out well, because they were so desperate they said they would have him anyway and let him play whatever he could manage. He was made up about that. (Not sure I am - he is practising more and more now, and the noise is horrendous. I have taken to wearing earplugs while I read and write.)

So things have kind of worked out OK in the end. Aubrey and I are best friends again; Harris is happy; Finn is happy; the VTs know their place.

The only mortifying thing in my life at the moment is that my mum has a boyfriend.

But the way she is smiling right now, I think I can live with that.

About the Author

Anna Wilson used to edit children's books until she discovered it was much more fun to write them. She took a flying leap from being an editor to being a fully-fledged author in 2008 and has never looked back (except when she has tripped over something). Inspired by her family, friends and pets, she writes funny yet heart-warming novels which are absolutely NOT based on any MORTIFYINGLY EMBARRASSING incidents which have happened to her in the past.*

Anna lives in Bradford on Avon with her husband, two children and an array of pets including a dog, cats, a tortoise and a pair of extremely noisy ducks.

*This may not be entirely true.